NEW RULES FOR REPROBATES

NEW RULES FOR REPROBATES

DEAD EVIL MERCENARY CORPS™ BOOK 6

MICHAEL ANDERLE

All of the characters, organizations, and events portrayed in this novel are either products of the author's imagination or are used fictitiously. Sometimes both.

LMBPN Publishing
PMB 196, 2540 South Maryland Pkwy
Las Vegas, NV 89109

Version 1.00, September 2022
ebook ISBN: 979-8-88541-772-3
Paperback ISBN: 979-8-88541-773-0

THE NEW RULES FOR REPROBATES TEAM

Thanks to our Beta Team:
John Ashmore, Rachel Beckford, Kelly O'Donnell, Malyssa Brannon

JIT Readers

Peter Manis
Dave Hicks
Jeff Goode
John Ashmore
Kelly O'Donnell
Zacc Pelter

Editor

SkyFyre Editing Team

DEDICATION

REMEMBERING JUDAH RAINE

Judah was a very strong advocate for the Zoo, a Sci Fi Universe created by Michael Anderle. (Why travel to a distant star system when you can visit an alien jungle here on Earth?). Judah took it upon herself to create an author's guide to help new authors to the Zoo get up-to-speed quickly. She enlisted several readers to help create the author guide, what she ultimately referred to as the "Zooclopedia tyrranica." It truly was a monster spreadsheet, which was appropriate for all of the alien mutant monsters that roamed the Zoo. We had a lot of fun creating mutant, hybrid monsters and coming up with crazy names for them.

Since the Zoo was surrounded by militaries from a number of different countries, we needed to research what military hardware and weapons each country would use to make the stories realistic. We're pretty sure that researching all the different weapons got us listed on a least one NSA watchlist - or three.

Besides being a reference for new Zoo authors, Judah

also played a key role in creating new stories for several, very popular Zoo series. She made the stories fast paced, entertaining and fun. Those books were always popular with our JIT proofreading group.

Hashing out Zoo storylines, mutant alien monsters and technology was a lively affair generating lengthy on-line discussions. Due to the time differences, those discussions usually didn't start until after 10:00PM Eastern time and could last until 1:00 or 2:00 AM. After a while, my wife made me mute the channel so she could sleep. (I guess that was better than her telling me to go to another room.)

Judah always showed her compassion, wit and sharp intellect during our discussions. She challenged us, grounded us and supported us so we could help the new authors and help make the Zoo stories the most entertaining and fun stories they could be.

I'll never forget our late night discussions, Judah's compassion, drive and wit and our Zoo family that grew out of our common interest in this Sci Fi Universe. She will be missed.

Written by John Ashmore, a valued member of the LMBPN Beta and JIT teams.

CHAPTER ONE

Dealing with the Bugz had taken some getting used to. The Scourge had its own challenges, but they weren't too unsettling, in her opinion. Wrecking the bots felt odd, but not enough to stick in her brain.

The mutants were something else, though.

Chill had no idea what might have caused them, where they had come from, or why they were acting the way they were. She didn't know much about how biological agents acted. While she'd heard that most of modern human history had been guided by planets of origin being decimated by biological agents, no one had much fear of using the damn things. Hell, as the stories went, humans had been driven off *their* planet of origin by biological agents. That hadn't changed anyone's mind about them.

The Dahin hadn't had that problem, so they wouldn't have learned the same lessons. They had a lot more excuses than humans did.

"I'm telling you," Chill muttered, drawing her knife. "One day, we will find ourselves easy-ass work helping people, with no adverse moral implications and a hell of a lot of creds paid into our account. A cushy job where we don't end up fighting monsters."

Kortez tilted his head and watched her. "What in our time together gives you the slightest inkling we'll be doing anything like that in the near future?"

She shrugged. "It's simple physics. Every action has an equal and opposite reaction, which means that since we've been putting ourselves up against the worst and the ugliest the galaxy has to offer, we're bound to come upon some good luck in the future to balance our bad luck."

"I don't think that's how physics works," Ivan noted. He checked his knives one last time. "For one thing, there's no such thing as luck when it comes to physics. Equal and opposite reaction does not apply in this situation."

Chill grinned. "Well, I don't care. There's an element of spirituality in my understanding of the universe and physics, so to my mind, all the bad shit that's happened to us lately means we're going to have good shit happening to us soon."

"But if good and bad are a matter of perspective," Kortez chimed in, "you'll have to put time and effort into making sure that whatever the universe sends you is good for *you*, not just for the majority of the universe."

"You're overthinking this." She shook her head as she ran a whetstone across her knife's blade. Her suit's HUD was useful for ensuring the edge was straight and as sharp as she could make it.

"You're *under*thinking this," Ivan shot back. "Waiting for the universe to give you good shit will let bad shit keep happening to you. You have to be the change you want to see in the universe."

"That's bullshit, and you know it. I'm not waiting for good shit to happen, anyway. We're all working our collective asses off, knowing all our hard work is eventually going to pay dividends and allow us to have our pick of what we want to do later on. Hopefully, we'll all still be alive and more or less intact by that time, but that's what we have coming to us."

"So, you're saying that once we've paid our dues in the merc business and made ourselves as popular as we can through the vid thing, we can get paid for working decent jobs that don't have us dealing with monsters galore?"

"Something like that. See, equal and opposite reaction."

Talking to them was better than keeping it all in her head. She was brooding too much, and it was good to get those thoughts out of her head. Share them so the rest of the crew could brood with her. She'd watched a bunch of vids, promotional material from security companies who were always looking for new and exciting talent to add to their rosters.

She'd been contacted by the recruiters for those companies, generic cold-messages saying they'd spotted the crew and liked their résumé. Would they come in for an interview at their earliest convenience?

Those security companies hired their mercs to corps looking to start wars without inciting them. That or had them babysitting a bunch of rich fucks who wanted to have muscle on their side when they started *their* wars. Chill didn't want any part of that, especially since they would be the newest crew. They would get the worst assignments until they'd proven themselves.

It also meant they would need to work for terrible people without questioning them. Chill wouldn't commit to that. Maybe after word got out to the proper folks about what they were doing on the Serpent and what their skillset was, they would get better offers. Not easy work, just the sort that wouldn't see them charging into the teeth of monster infestations every other day.

That, or they would end up with enough creds so they could set themselves up in business. The kind that would let them make money without needing to risk their lives.

All mercs had more or less the same dream. A few got more specific, saying they were only working the merc job so they could get the money to buy land to farm, or support a family business that was struggling on their home planet.

Interestingly, those were the people who ended up dying early. Precious few got the number of creds they needed and retired. Chill never heard from them again unless they had to get back to working the merc business, usually because they'd lost all the creds they'd saved and needed to start over.

That wasn't the way. Mercs had to focus. After they had the creds to spend, they could start thinking about what they were going to spend them on.

"All right, we have assholes on approach," Kortez alerted them. "Like the last fucking mutant wave wasn't enough. Shit's worse than the Scourge."

"Never thought I would say this, but I miss the Scourge," Ivan muttered, flicking one of his knives into the air and catching it deftly. "I mean, they're still out and about on the station, but I miss fighting them."

"I don't think we're missing the Scourge." Chill hefted her rifle. She kept Blitz's hammer on her belt, although she knew Kortez wanted to get his hands on it. "We just don't like dealing with those fucking mutants."

Those fucking mutants. The three words which had been a theme in the week since the arch-nest had been destroyed. It had left them with a diminished bot force to hold the mutants back. Piles of bots were popping up all over the place, which revealed the size of the workforce they could have utilized had the arch-nest been left intact.

Chill still had doubts about whether the AI running the Scourge could be trusted. For the moment, they didn't have much choice in the matter. The mutants were the new threat, and they had to deal with them.

"Wave coming in from the left side," Chill alerted, highlighting the points the creepers were approaching from. "Oh, on the right side too. Looks like they're ganging up on us."

"So, just like the last time." Ivan started setting up mines to deal with the corridors they weren't covering. "You think the Janissaries will need our help again?"

Chill shook her head. "Fuckers know they get churned up when they go against the Janissaries. They're probing for our weak points."

The mutants didn't know how to handle the human crews. They probably didn't know much about the Janissaries either. They were, however, showing the kind of intelligent decision-making she'd seen from other sentient beings, and they sometimes acted smarter.

In other ways, they were stupid. Chill could not understand why they didn't collect the weapons of the people they had killed. They didn't use armor either, though they threw themselves at their opponents. But like with the Scourge and the Bugz, there seemed to be an intelligence driving them forward.

They infested those they killed. She'd seen the creepers drag away the bodies of the fallen, which were swallowed by the plant life. There was no sign of rotting or decay in the bodies, so the mutation kept the bodies alive and well to do their bidding.

The first of them crossed her path, and Chill pulled the trigger by instinct and reflex. That was the trick to help her shoot more accurately.

Kortez and Ivan fired as well, picking up on advances through the other passages. Chill had selected the spot because eight halls came together there. They were practically daring the mutants to attack from many points, offering them what they would think was an easy target.

She was starting to understand how the mutants thought. They were getting bolder and pushing deeper into Scourge territory. There was still some fight to the Scourge, but less as time went on. Every day, they saw fewer bots and more creepers.

One less now. The rifle round punched through its neck and collarbone, blowing the head off. There was no telling why they dropped when their heads were blown off since the creepers were long since dead, but it worked.

A few days of trial and error—as well as blasting off different body parts on different creatures to get the right one—had revealed shots to the chest didn't do much damage. Damaging or knocking their legs off was effective. Even though they were dead, they still needed those to move around. It didn't kill them, but limiting their mobility was an important part of keeping the swarms from rushing in too quickly.

Chill was willing to accept that as a part of the fight. They had learned early that when they were dealing with smaller groups, headshots would bring them down. With waves, shooting at the legs was the way to go. Shooting at the neck did the same thing as shooting the head. Since she had been aiming for the head and missed, she would take the kill. More of them were slipping through, letting out the dull moan they used to communicate. She shifted her aim lower and opened fire.

Her rifle quickly started to overheat, so she switched over to the other one. Those missing their legs were still clawing forward. A few managed to climb over their fallen comrades, still moaning and hissing.

Kortez and Ivan were as busy as she was. They were covering other points of attack, which prevented them from supporting her against the fuckers who were getting too close to her.

While she was switching rifles, one of the creepers grabbed her leg. She kicked it away, but three more took its place. Chill pulled out Blitz's hammer to deal with them while sending a steady stream of tungsten rounds down the hall she was responsible for clearing.

The hammer was an effective tool in close-quarters combat, though Chill wasn't convinced that it was better than her knife. It could crush anything in front of her, but she needed space to swing it. The knife didn't need as much space. It could be stabbed to get in under armor, while a hammer couldn't.

Still, the hammer cleared out the creepers moving toward her from below. Its inertia generator punched chunks off of the creatures, raining blood and gore across the walls. The impacts left little for them to attack her with. Chill took a step back, keeping the shots flowing and firing through the corpses of creepers that charged her.

She couldn't see the other crews, although she kept her eye on the pulsating markers that told her they were all alive and still in business. She didn't know if they had been engaged by the mutants or were moving down their assigned routes. They were all in territories that had formerly been held by the Scourge.

It was now about who could grab the positions the fastest. Chill had identified the vital locations that would be the most difficult for them to take, and they had attacked those in the first few days. They had let what was left of the Scourge do most of the fighting while they consolidated their position. From there, it was a slow, deliberate process of pushing the mutants back while maintaining a safe point for the advance troops to fall back to.

They had needed it on multiple occasions. They had vastly underestimated the mutants' numbers.

"Looks like that's all they sent our way," Kortez growled, checking his rifle as Ivan tossed a grenade down his hall to clear the rest of them out.

They were retreating quickly and seemed to know the station better than anyone. Every time the mercs tried to press their advantage, the retreating critters found a tunnel or service access that allowed them to slip away. Almost like they hadn't been there in the first place. They were covered in green and black foliage, with the roots under their skin taking on a pattern. It looked almost like war paint. Primal.

If they were intelligent, they didn’t show it, but there was something slippery about the bastards that chilled her more than the bots ever had. They could travel anywhere in the station using the same ways they retreated, yet they attacked in ways that allowed them to be intercepted, stopped, and repelled. They had won several engagements —that was what Chill assumed it meant when a couple of the decky crews went missing—but they never left any bodies.

Nothing to indicate that they were pressing forward.

"You think they're taking the bodies?"

Ivan and Kortez turned to peer down the tunnel she'd been defending, tilting their heads. "Don't think so," Kortez answered. "Still, we wouldn't want them to take what we killed, recycle it, and send it at us. Might be time for us to institute a policy to burn all the bodies we leave behind so they can't get back up."

"How would we do that?" Ivan asked. "We don't have any flamethrowers, and incendiary grenades are expensive. I mean, I'm sure we could find a burner room in the station, but do we want to put ourselves through the trouble of dragging the corpses there to be cremated?"

"We wouldn't have to ash them. Whatever this mutation is, it needs the bodies to be functional, so all we need to do is disable them. We could do a good job of that by wrecking the legs and arms, but we don't know what the hell it does to those bodies or if it can heal the damage. We could carry accelerant in our packs, and when we're done fighting, spray and burn them. That'll keep them from popping right the fuck up when we turn our backs."

"That wasn't what I was talking about," Chill cut in. "Although that wouldn't be the worst idea. No, I was wondering what they did with the bodies of the people they killed, and where all the bodies they're working with now are coming from. Might be the Dahin from years past. You know, the ones who used to inhabit the station. Maybe deckies who disappeared back in the day."

Kortez nodded. "Something like that. It's nightmare-inducing that we're fighting our own comrades who are brought back from the dead. You think that's an intentional move?"

"It is psychotic," Chill commented. "Although, the people who designed the biological agent might have had that in mind." The situation would be worse if they thought about who they were shooting. If they hesitated, they died.

She took a deep breath and shifted her focus as they moved back to where they could hear shooting. None of the others had sent up distress signals yet, but Ivan had set up mines in their sector to make sure the creepers couldn't come up behind them without warning.

There *was* the chance of them losing the area of the Vert where the explosives went off, but they were past worrying about that.

She was done with the Serpent. They would only die here for someone else's inheritance. She thought they could do better elsewhere.

She wondered how the rest of the crew would take her

new and improved point of view. Maybe the Jindahin should just blow the hell out of the station and build a new one. They were going to end up spending more money to retake it than it was worth.

Then again, it had probably cost quadrillions of creds. That was assuming they could lash the three suns to the station again if the first one was destroyed. So, maybe not. There were too many unknowns and variables to keep them from making large-scale decisions about the station until they knew more about what they were facing.

"Yeah, I know," Chill growled, noting that her two crew-mates were staring at her as they reached another group. They had just wrapped up a raid, and they would rejoin the crew led by Shoviil.

"You think there's going to be lots more attacks?" Ivan wondered aloud, studying the corpses the mutants had left behind. "I mean, fighting through every inch of the Vert will take us a while, and no one will get much done if we have to worry about monsters popping out at us."

Chill didn't comment. She had her own opinion on the matter. If anyone else wanted to bail, they were going to get to that opinion on their own.

Besides, they had to check the dead mutants. They weren't fond of tech-based weapons, which wasn't to say they didn't have defenses. She had seen them waving chunks of metal or prefab that had been sharpened to make them deadlier. However, they'd never taken the weapons from the bodies. Hell, she'd seen one of them pick up a rifle someone had dropped and use it as a club instead of shooting it.

Chill couldn't understand why they didn't use the

weapons they retrieved as intended. They seemed intent on staying in the Stone Age despite all the tech around them. However, they had set the station's life support so it actively encouraged growth and had a lot of humidity in the atmo. They used tech in other ways as well, but most of them had slipped her mind. It was interesting, though.

She dropped to her haunches and inspected one of the larger bodies that had been taken over by the mutation. Thick, corded roots rippled through it like veins, and it was difficult to tell what species the person had been.

More importantly, this one had armor.

"Kortez, come take a look at this." She waved him over, moving chunks of flesh and brain matter off the spot she was looking at on the creature's chest. "Is that armor?"

Kortez inspected the spot on the creature's chest. "That looks like a sheet of aluminum that has been...yep, bolted into the chest. Would be painful if these creatures felt pain. That sheet would deflect caster rounds better than skin and bones. I guess it would stop knives too. It didn't do much to stop rifle rounds, though. Yeah, it counts as armor, and since the critter added it, it intentionally tried to defend itself."

"Well, if that isn't just fucking special." Ivan crossed his arms. "Wait, how do you know the damn thing didn't have it on when he started?"

Chill knew the answer. "You'd see scar tissue around the bolts." There were traditions that called for self-mutilation and attaching objects to one's person. Mostly among the Suids, who had a tradition of attaching armor to themselves. She'd looked it up when they'd picked Dorian up and seen a lot she didn't want to see.

"Exactly," Kortez agreed. "No scar tissue around the bolts means it's fairly recent. Something the mutant did to be more durable."

Shoviil noticed them as he was gathering his troops and enthusiastically waved for them to approach. "We've been fighting everywhere. Seems like the mutants are probing our defenses. Hopefully, we didn't give them a good look at what we're doing, so they ended up with nothing to show for all their losses."

"You're really upbeat," Ivan pointed out.

"Well, the Scourge is not a problem anymore." Shoviil looked around. "Most of the deckies are working together now, and we're going up against a new threat. I don't know; it feels like it's a new day around here. We had a couple new merc teams show up and join the fight, so everything's looking up."

That was one way to look at it. Maybe if you had been dealing with the Scourge for decades, the mutants weren't so terrible.

"New mercs, huh?" Kortez looked around. "Are we taking any steps to make sure none of them pull what the Hammers and the Harvest did?"

"We'll be watching to see if they get homicidal," Chill assured him.

It was obvious who the new guys were. Those who had been on the station for a while had stomachs of steel. Those used to dealing with the weird, the bizarre, and sometimes, the sickening. The new ones looked green around the gills and might have been wondering if this was the right career path.

"Don't worry," Chill assured some new mercs as she

approached. "When the systems are up and running, they deal with the garbage. It won't smell as bad while you're setting up a defensive perimeter."

One of the greenhorns took a step forward. He wasn't human, but Chill couldn't tell his race under the heavy armor. "Didn't...didn't there used to be a lot of people on this station?"

Kortez dragged Cortador out of the chest of a body he was making sure was dead. "As best we can figure. Nobody's checked to see if they are getting it on in their creeper holes."

"When referring to creeper holes," Ivan interrupted, "what kind of hole are we talking about?"

"I think I'm going to be sick," another of the newcomers muttered.

Chill shrugged. "Take off your helmet, and the cleaning protocols will take care of that too."

CHAPTER TWO

"You ever think the people who wanted to take this station down knew something we don't?" Kortez asked.

"Hmm?" Chill narrowed her eyes. "What are you talking about?"

"Well, they attacked this place over and over, right?" Kortez rolled his shoulders as they approached Coil Cove. "I'm wondering if they might have had a point, considering the bullshit we've been with."

"The tale we got from the authorities isn't adding up." Ivan flicked one of his knives into the air and caught it by the blade. "What we've been dealing with is the result of that Lugosh fellow screwing his retirement plan up, not people attacking the station."

Kortez nodded. "I get that, but we're looking at a place that's clearly cursed. Maybe it's too close to the nebula or something, but everyone who had put time and effort into this place has suffered for it."

"Wait." Chill raised a hand to stop that train of thought

before it left the station. "You're saying that because bad shit happened, the station is cursed?"

"Do you disagree? I mean, there's bad luck, and then there's fucking being cursed."

Chill shook her head. "I don't believe in curses. If anywhere in the galaxy is, it's Mugh-9, but all we're looking at here is natural entropy."

"It can be both."

"It can, but it probably isn't."

"You know," Ivan interjected, "with all the crazy crap you've seen, you'd think you would be less of a skeptic. There's weird shit out there that you can't fully understand."

Kortez nodded. "We've been out and about for a while. Some people are just fucking cursed. So are places and ships. Ask a group of long-haul sailors. They're superstitious fuckers. Spend a couple of months with them, and you'll end up believing shit you wouldn't consider right now. My point is, you can't rule anything out."

"You would want solid evidence of magical curses on stations, planets, and people before you make any life choices based on them." Chill raised an eyebrow. "Believe whatever the hell you want. I just won't share it."

"Right." Ivan grinned. "It's not like believing in ghosts."

"Who believes in ghosts?" Chill asked.

"Shoviil was talking about them communing with the ghosts of the fallen the other day," Kortez explained.

"Oh. Well, again, he can believe whatever he wants."

She wasn't skeptical about everything. She just couldn't help the feeling that their questions, direct and indirect, were just them trying to figure out more about her. She wasn't going to make it easy for them. She was a very private person, and besides, there were downsides to letting the galaxy know everything about her. She wanted to keep everyone guessing.

"Changing the subject," she began. Subtlety had never been her strong suit. "We are drawing a lot more talent to the station. Kortez had a point when he brought up avoiding the situation we had with the Hammers and the Harvest."

"You pointed out that we can't control who comes here," Ivan reminded her. "It might be nice to play gods, but there's nothing we can do aside from giving them work and hoping they're happy with it."

"Well, there's a station's worth of work waiting for them." Kortez gestured around as they approached the ships that had docked in their absence. None of them were well-put-together, but the people disembarking looked upbeat. Simple mercs, the sort who weren't looking for politics. They just wanted to shoot things and be paid a fair wage for doing it.

The Over-Keeper was more than willing to drop creds on them. Chill thought he was being generous because he would have a large number of creds coming his way from the treasure he would be inheriting. That, or the Jindahin officials who were financing the project had seen taking care of the Scourge as progress, even if they *had* unleashed something worse. They might have decided to loosen the purse strings.

"Anyway." She shook her head. "Progress is being made on the reclamation sites on the other Verts. Dorian, are these data markers right?"

"Oh... Didn't... Hey, guys! How was dealing with the mutant fuckers?"

"Did I catch you napping?" Chill asked, raising an eyebrow.

"Napping would be less embarrassing." Dorian cleared his throat. "Uh, yeah. The data markers are the most recent ones we have. Even with the number of Scourge dropping, we can still access their server nodes to stay in touch with the station. It'll take a while to get it all up and running, and we're going to have to manually activate the nodes in what used to be the nests. Even then, from what I'm reading, we'll only be able to access the basic internal workings of the servers. Everything else will be down until we get experts to work on it."

"Yeah, I talked to Kuzratha. He's not sure if they even have the access codes to repair the software." Ivan scowled. "We have to yank all the hardware out and install something from this century."

"They're not bringing anyone official here until we clear the station," Chill reminded them. "Which means we can't bring the station online until later. I've been wondering if the mutants are tech-savvy. If they're not, we're dealing with something that is since they set up life support wherever they go."

"Is that the kind of thing you brood about?" Kortez asked. "That's actually a good thought."

"About damn time she had a good thought," Ivan growled. "She spends enough time spaced out."

"Yeah, it's called thinking," Chill countered. "The pair of you might want to try it."

"Too much work." Kortez shook his head. "Besides, that's what we have you for."

"That's why you annoy me about it too, I guess." Chill grinned. "Still, the new mercs come to us to find out how we're going to work through the station. It feels like they're fucking treating us like, I don't know, the directors of a growing confederation of mercs."

"I thought it was a good idea to pair each new merc crew with a decky crew," Ivan remarked. "None of us knows what we're dealing with, not even the deckies. This way, the new guys aren't on their own out there."

She'd come up with that idea, but Shoviil had implemented it. He knew the decky crews best. He sometimes fought with the crews, but most of his time was spent coordinating the teams alongside the Over-Keeper to get an idea of how much each of the teams was worth.

Alex had given them Chill's algorithm. It had to be updated for their current situation, but it was helping everyone get paid decently and on time. She hadn't been paid extra for it. No complaints since they were receiving more now than when they had been dealing with the Scourge. She wouldn't be greedy.

"Good to have extra people," Chill muttered as they reached the ship nearest theirs. "We're going to need as many guns as we can clear to fight the mutants."

"The hell kind of ship is that?" Kortez asked. "Looks like an Authority ship, but those engines are human-made. The thrusters, anyway."

"Most of these mercs weren't mobile," Chill reminded him. "When they hear about a decent place to work, they buy or lease a cheap vessel to get to that place. Sometimes they get a loan from a bank to buy a ship, but it's nothing long-term."

"Why didn't we get a loan like that?" Ivan tilted his head. "I remember our first ship, and it almost got us killed."

"Because I thought we could survive on something that could get us out of atmo. Looking back, I should have known that you get what you pay for when it comes to ships. Or who you kill to get one."

Their current ship was a lot better than what *they* could have afforded. They had taken it from some mercs who had tried to kill them.

"Right." Ivan shrugged. "Still, seems like they don't think they're going to have to make the return journey. Doesn't look like the ship *can* make the return journey."

Chill grinned. "All right, let's go home. We have more work to do before we're down for the day shift."

Chill would admit that things felt better. A massive weight had been lifted off her shoulders and mind. She was now convinced that the Scourge had perpetrated a psychological effect on the whole of the station that had constantly preyed on their psyches. Now that it was gone, she didn't feel the same way about the Serpent.

"No." Kortez shook his head and continued his conversation with Ivan. Chill, lost in thought, wasn't following it. "You don't have to get a ship from a dealer. It's better to do that, but you can buy one from any seller. It's better to get it through a dealer since they have to prep the ship for sale. That was how we ended up with that piece of crap."

"Picking one up from a dealer is more expensive," Ivan countered. "The commissions they put on top of the cost of the ship, plus the repairs and taxes. Sometimes, it's better to buy direct. You have to know a thing or two about how ships work and make sure you're not stuck with a lemon like we were, but if you're a discerning buyer, you can do well."

"That's the problem. We were anything but discerning buyers."

"Sorry to interrupt," Dorian interrupted. "The Over-Keeper wants to have a word with you. He was keeping an eye on the local feeds and waiting for you guys to come back. He asks that you come to his antechamber whenever you have the time. He's not going to wait for you, though."

Chill sighed, shaking her head. "Right. We'll head over there."

"We?" Kortez asked, narrowing his eyes. "I thought—"

"You thought wrong if you thought you're going to leave me to deal with that asshole alone. Now, get out of your suits. Then we'll go find out what the Over-Keeper wants."

CHAPTER THREE

It had taken some doing, but the area around the antechamber leading into the vault had quickly become one of the most secure spots on the station. Chill wasn't sure how many people had been involved in the building, but that was where the Over-Keeper spent most of his creds.

She knew why he was making that call. It had the most functional systems on the station. The AI was still working, even with the rest of the Scourge gone, although he only spoke when Kuzratha was around.

Turrets had been set up at every juncture, ready to turn anything that got its hackles up into a fine red mist. There were sectors rigged to blow and cave the structure in to hold the antechamber.

Chill believed Kuzratha would have turned it into the central staging area for the other teams to move through. Problem was, he didn't want a bunch of greedy mercs hanging around the spot where his treasure would be delivered after the station was secured.

If it ever was. Chill was willing to be supportive and optimistic to a point, but it was a big station, and they hadn't even explored a quarter of it. It was looking like the kind of job that could take decades to complete, if they ever did.

The Over-Keeper might end up dead. Then the funding would dry up, and all the mercs would drift off to places where they could get paid. They wouldn't be left with much for their efforts, and the deckies would be left to deal with the mutant infestation on their own.

Until someone else decided it was worth the time and effort to pour millions of creds into retaking the station. Then it would happen all again. She suspected this was not the Over-Keeper's first attempt at retaking the Serpent, or not his family's first attempt. Considering his knowledge of what they were looking for, she thought it was a possibility. He didn't want them to have a good idea of what they were looking at or what they were doing.

It pissed her off, but Chill was learning to pick up on what the Over-Keeper was trying to keep from them and making sure he knew that *she* knew he was doing it.

That was the best way for them to operate if he was going to keep his secrets. The best part was that he lost it whenever he thought they were hiding something. He had cannibalized a significant portion of his ship to set his forces up with defenses they had full control over. That had killed his chance of leaving the station if there was an emergency.

Kuzratha was fully committed to seeing this through, regardless of how it played out.

"You know, I've heard he's not even letting the Janissaries spend much time here," Ivan pointed out, tapping on one of the doors to let the Over-Keeper know they were waiting for him. "Seems like the guy is getting paranoid and doesn't even trust his own people."

"They're not his people," Chill reminded him. "They're still sworn to the Salifate, which means that if they're ordered by their superiors to cut their losses and leave, they will. Kuzratha understands that better than anyone else, so he's preparing for the eventuality that he'll have to further his ambitions alone."

Ivan shrugged. "Seems like all that could have been avoided if he trusted people more."

"It's against his nature. He's probably got an intelligence background, so he's of the opinion that knowledge is power. He's not going to be willing to share that power unless he's getting something in return."

Kortez cleared his throat and looked around the room they were waiting in. "You think he's listening in on this conversation?"

"Of that, I have no doubt," Chill answered with a small smile. "It's good for him to know how we feel about him. That way, he knows what'll happen if he fucks with us again."

As if on cue, the door hissed open, allowing them deeper into the antechamber. There were more security checkpoints and plenty of ways for the Over-Keeper to defend himself from attacks, not only from the mutants but also from anyone else who wanted to steal his treasure.

It was overkill for dealing with what was essentially a bunch of savages swinging clubs. It meant either he was covering hidden knowledge of the capabilities of those savages, or he was expecting there to be another attack from the mercs or the deckies—or both.

Either scenario had merit, Chill supposed, although she might just be paranoid.

"I mean, you have to give it to the guy." Kortez looked around. "He has put a lot of work into making this place into a fortress. I wish we could have pulled it off."

"Pulled what off?"

The Janissaries' commander was approaching from one of the side halls.

"We were just talking about the security you put into this area." She offered her hand to the Dahin in greeting, and he almost didn't notice it.

He did take it and shake it awkwardly after a few seconds. He still wasn't comfortable with human greeting traditions.

"After what happened with the Harvest, the Over-Keeper doesn't trust only two of my men to keep his treasure safe." Kharkanaw looked around the chamber, then chuckled. "He could have just had the Janissaries defend the Vert, but I suppose he wanted to have my men and me available to you at the other points of attack."

Kharkanaw knew that was bullshit. That, or he was tired of being ordered around by the Over-Keeper. The Janissaries lived by their own code, and they and the DEMC were going to have to work together despite their cultural differences.

They *were* getting the Janissaries to see them as more than simple tools to be swung at the nearest threat.

"If he was only anticipating a threat from the mutants, it wouldn't need heavy firepower like this," Kharkanaw continued, motioning for them to follow him. "You would need ways to funnel them into choke points, then plenty of crowd control elements. I would set up some access points to vent the atmo and let whatever's inside die that way. It would be a good way to stop the mutants. Maybe less effective in dealing with armored mercs.

"The armor, the turrets, and the drones are in place to make sure none of the mercs or the deckies try to cause more trouble. Those kinds of measures are called for. Given the actions of the Sempers, the Hammers, and the Harvest, we have to keep those people at arm's length."

Those people. The Janissaries saw the mercs as lesser, but it was tough to be reminded of that when it felt like they were making progress with the group. Sometimes they acted like another crew that was there to make a living. Then the commander dropped one of those lines, which reminded them of how they were viewed by their putative reclamation partners.

"Then again," Chill cut in, changing the subject, "there is a lot more to the mutants than we think. Fighting the ones that are just throwing themselves at our defenses is one thing. I can't help thinking there's more to the infestation than we're giving them credit for."

"What makes you say that?"

"They know how to keep the life support on when the Scourge was turning it off. That indicates they're more intelligent than the front-line troops would make us think."

Kharkanaw nodded like that was not new information.

Chill frowned. "You've got a weird look on your face." Even by Dahin standards, the Janissaries were oddities, genetically modified to turn them into real juggernauts. That also made them difficult to get a bead on.

"I don't know." He crossed his arms. "We've been dealing with these creatures almost on a daily basis, and we have seen some oddities. They are communicating with something, maybe an intelligence that is staying away from us. Nothing we can do to stop them without a full campaign into the Verts they control, but a couple of days ago, I thought I saw creatures that were different.

"Almost covered in the plant stuff, unlike the others, which only have it growing in their veins. They were shouting what sounded like orders. The rest were avoiding being anywhere close to where they were standing, circling around them. I saw one of them kneel when it got too close like it was apologizing for its disrespect."

Chill brought their troop to a halt. "You've seen this happen? Like, with your own eyes?"

Kharkanaw nodded. "With my own eyes, and I caught it on vid on my HUD. I'll see about getting it over to you. There's more to these mutants than we think. There's a reason why even the Scourge wasn't able to clear them out, and between us and the Gorzar, there should have been no contest between the bots and the mutants.

"I would bet my own creds that the infestation managed to alter the core coding of the Scourge to make it focus more on the deckies and us than on clearing it out."

She wasn't willing to go that far. Chill had seen strange shit on the station, but if she was going to start thinking a biological weapon was capable of coding, she was going to need more evidence to support it. It was a great plot twist for a vid.

"Don't bother, Commander," Kortez cut in. "You're dealing with quite the skeptic in Chill here. If you want her to think there's something to your little theory, you'll need three or four years of studies and super computers running sims for her to even consider it as a possibility."

"It's not an irrational position to hold," Chill countered. "But that's not the point. We're already dealing with shit nobody's ever seen, so we're in unknown waters anyway. We need to be cautious and keep our minds open about what we might be running into."

That wasn't the answer Kortez had been expecting. He regarded her for a moment before nodding.

"Unknown waters." Kharkanaw tilted his head and grinned. "I don't think I've heard that particular term before."

"Really? You'd think the Dahin would use it." Chill paused. "Unless I'm being insensitive. How do the Dahin feel about people talking about their aquatic origins?"

The commander shrugged his massive shoulders. "People who care about that kind of shit spend too much time commenting on vids and too little time in the real world."

That got a grin from Chill. She studied the defenses they were approaching. The area outside the antechamber had once been covered in greenery that came straight out of the prefab. It had been cleared out, and chunks of the prefab had been torn up to get rid of anything that would open them up to the possibility of the monsters making their way back in.

Chill could understand being careful, but they had left a

great deal of destruction behind while turning a civilized if overgrown hallway into a warzone.

Everything had been cleared out of the area to remove obstructions so the plasma cannons that had been set up behind some armor could rain bolts on attackers. It was the heaviest of the defenses they'd seen so far, and there would be no attacking it outright. They would have to find a way to deactivate those cannons or anything that attacked would be turned into molten slag.

"Right," Kharkanaw muttered, gesturing at the door. "It's in there. Doors should be open, and he'll be waiting for you."

"Who controls the turrets?" Chill asked, raising an eyebrow. "Seems like the effort might be beyond our man on the hill."

"Nobody, as far as I know," he answered. "Might be that AI, but I doubt even he would be that stupid."

"Oh, I don't know," Chill muttered. "People do the craziest shit in the name of maintaining their personal riches. Good to see you again, Commander. We won't keep you any longer."

The massive Dahin tapped his heels together in his military's equivalent of a salute, then went on his way.

"Right." She glared at the cannons before moving ahead of the rest of her team. "Let's go see how the Over-Keeper is feeling this afternoon."

CHAPTER FOUR

"Good afternoon, Over-Keeper," Chill began. She spoke loudly as she looked around for a sign that they were in the right place.

Considering the firepower she had seen, Chill didn't want to risk startling their host and accidentally getting pulverized. If she was going to be killed, she wanted it to be an intentional act by Kuzratha. She was hoping that wouldn't be the case either.

"Chill, good of you to come meet me." The Over-Keeper looked up from a desk he was leaning over. Despite the richness of his robes, it looked like he had been wearing them for a while. He looked disheveled, which Chill had never seen before. "I take it your ventures against the infestations were successful?"

"We had some tough fights, but we pushed the mutants back without much effort," Chill answered truthfully. "I doubt it'll stay this easy, though."

"I believe you are correct in that assumption." The Treasure Keeper made a holographic appearance next to the

Over-Keeper. The pair had spent more time with each other than with anyone else over the past week or so. While Chill appreciated the amount of work Kuzratha was putting into finding out more about the station, spending most of his time with an AI was odd.

Dorian would do that, not a high-level actor for the Jindahin Salifate. Then again, Chill was more suspicious of the AI than the others on her team, so it might have to do with that.

"Can't say I've had to deal with an unknown to this extent, though," Chill continued. The Over-Keeper was lost in thought again. "The intelligence our AI friend here had provided has been invaluable, but if you have anything else to add to our knowledge, we would appreciate it. Going in with all the intelligence we have is a great way to save lives."

"I agree." The Over-Keeper nodded and motioned for them to take a seat next to the table he was working at. "I've been deciphering the data on the biological agents we've run into, but I'm seeing only lore and legend. It appears that Lugosh didn't know much about what he was stealing. I also have to work my way through what the AI is allowed to tell me about the matter. It would have been better if he had saved it on a regular server."

"I apologize for the inconvenience," the AI interjected with a smile. "Please let me know if there is anything else I can assist you with."

Kuzratha glared at the AI. That look told Chill he'd heard that line too often. There wasn't much he could do to change it until the station was cleared and ready to be used, though.

"Unfortunately, the bad news does not end there." The Over-Keeper delicately brushed his fingers over his clothing as if he realized it wasn't in the state he would have wanted. "Word has gotten back to the Salifate's command about our progress. While we have done a great deal more than was ever expected from this operation, I'm afraid their reception of the news was tempered by the state of the war."

Chill hadn't been following the fighting. They had access to the feeds and the cast networks in the station, but she hadn't had the time to follow the news cycles in the rest of the galaxy. Most of her downtime was either spent researching topics that could help them or watching older vids. Those were what she queued up when she needed to relax before bed.

"War's not going too well for them, eh?" Kortez chimed in with a chuckle. "Although I guess they shouldn't be calling it a war anymore, right? Ceasefire and all that."

He stopped talking when the Over-Keeper fixed him with the same glare he'd directed at the AI moments before.

"We have to show the Salifate command more results than we've seen so far." Kuzratha raised an eyebrow. "They are running out of time and funds and therefore patience over our current progress, so they need the project to move on to the next phase. Otherwise, we might see them take matters into their own hands."

"So, you brought us here to tell us we've been doing good work, but we need to do better," Ivan commented, crossing his arms. "That's the kind of thing someone says before killing someone else to get them out of the way."

"I don't think it will come to that." Kuzratha didn't sound convincing.

"But you *are* saying that despite pushing harder and faster into the station than anyone else has, you want us to commit more time, effort, and troops to fight an enemy we know next to nothing about in the hope of making your higher-ups think better of our situation here." Chill thought that summed the situation up well.

Maybe the Janissaries wouldn't mind it if the Dahin command decided they wanted someone else to take point on the mission. They had a great deal of respect and deference for the Over-Keeper, but maybe they wanted someone else to be in charge.

Likely someone with more military in their background.

Chill thought that might be a good idea. The change of tone aside, having people who were committed to clearing the station rather than profiting from it would be best in the long run. She wasn't going to say there were no downsides to the idea, however.

"What'll happen to the deckies and the mercs if that happens?" Chill asked, narrowing her eyes. "I mean, the whole idea behind sending us in to handle the situation on the station was to make sure none of the other interested parties knew the Jindahin were involved, right? Has that changed?"

"Not yet, but it might." The Over-Keeper slumped in his seat, looking more exhausted than she'd ever seen him. She might need to mention that he was spending too much time with the AI. "The circumstances might change. They might need the resources on this station, no matter who finds out about it, and they'll push to take it over before anyone can stop them.

“If that happens, the deckies and the mercenaries will just slow them down. The first thing the military will do is subjugate or kill everyone on the station who is not Jindahin in the name of securing the area. Resistance will be met with extreme force.”

Chill crossed her arms. "We don't know if those assholes are just going to do that anyway after we get the job done. If they're threatening to kick us out and will kill us if we don't agree, it might be better off if we just bail. Cut our losses."

She got sideways glances from Kortez and Ivan. Chill wanted to make it sound like she was negotiating instead of threatening to leave.

"Not to say that we're thinking of leaving, mind," she continued. "But if we'll eventually be dealing with the hardliners, we might as well let *them* retake the station. If I know hardliners, and I do, if they meet enough resistance from the Scourge, the infestation, or us, they'll just bomb the shit out of the station to make sure nobody else gets their grubby mitts on it. How close am I, Over-Keeper?"

Kuzratha stared at her, then shrugged. "Honestly? I'm not sure. The leadership is in flux at the moment. From what I'm told, between the losses they've suffered and the internal power struggle, who is running things changes from day to day. Your assumptions are on target. Too much time and money have been invested in building this station and retaking it, so they have to ensure the investment does not end up in the wrong hands."

"I'd say *their* hands are the wrong hands," Kortez

growled. "I'm starting to wonder why the fuck we're working for the Jindahin if they're going to kill us off the moment they decide they don't need us anymore."

"In fairness, I think a lot of the corps would make the same call," Ivan countered. "Although that's not a justification for the Jindahin. More a condemnation for the way most of the corps do business."

The Over-Keeper sighed. "From the point of view of the hardliners, they are fighting tooth and scale for their way of life. They see it as a justification for anything that needs to be done in the name of saving the Jindahin."

"You know we won't go along with that, right?" Chill took a step forward. "We commit to the jobs we take on, but if the circumstances change, we'll need to adjust the terms of our agreement. We did it with the Kahdahin, and we'll do it with you. If you start justifying their fucked-up shit, we'll pull our support."

"I understand that," Kuzratha snapped. "If you want to keep things peaceful, we'll have to keep them from launching an all-out attack on the station—or asteroid-bomb it. They gave me a timeline, which is the time it will take to get a fleet out here."

"Two weeks?" Chill asked after running the calculations in her head. "Maybe more."

"Give or take, yes. So we have two weeks to get the station operational."

Ivan snorted. "Might be better for us to duck out and let them try their hand at this bullshit. To get the wormhole up and running again, we'll have to clear a lot more of the Verts. Not all of them, mind, but taking over a majority of the station is one hell of a task. Even then, there won't be any guarantee they won't just clear us off the station, along with any of the mercs or deckies who are left over."

"I know what you're fishing for," Kuzratha muttered.

"Fishing? We're carpet-bombing." Kortez rolled his eyes. "We'll need assurances from you and the other Jindahin assholes that your first act after we retake the station for you isn't to space us."

"I thought you had gathered intelligence that would be detrimental to the Jindahin if there was such an attempt."

"We're going to need assurances anyway," Chill cut in before Kortez could say the Dahin didn't know what he was talking about. "We don't want to start any bad shit with you or the rest of the Salifate, and as long as everyone involved commits to finding a way to make it work, no further solutions are required."

"I have another solution," the Over-Keeper suggested. "One that involves clearing the station and thus unlocking Lugosh's treasure. I've been speaking to the AI, and among the many treasures inside the vault he is keeping in a side-space fluctuation is an original copy of the *Jin'Mak'Koh*."

"What is that?" Kortez looked around the antechamber. Most of the priceless artifacts that had been hung on the walls were still intact and present. "Another bit of fancy treasure everybody on your side wants?"

"In a manner of speaking." Kuzratha narrowed his eyes. "I'm trying, but I can't think of a human equivalent. None comes to mind. It is the holy writings upon which the Jindahin religion and culture were founded. With these documents in hand and my confirmed status as a descendant of Lugosh—who might have been a renegade but is remembered as a hero by most of the military families—I could make a play for leadership among the Jindahin remnant. With that, I could direct the fleet to use the wormhole while leaving the deckies and any mercenaries who remain on the station to operate it in a symbiotic relationship with those Jindahin who stick around."

Chill tilted her head and glanced at the other two members of her crew before nodding. "Interesting. Why do I think this plan was in the works before we ever set foot on the Serpent?"

"That's not possible," the Over-Keeper answered. "How could I have known it was a possibility then if I only found out about the presence of the *Jin'Mak'Koh* on the station after I spoke to the Treasure Keeper?"

They were apparently playing a game. "Supposing you didn't know about the text before we got here, which you'll forgive me for doubting, you would have had to know there was *something* on the station a clever and opportunistic fellow like you would find a way to use appropriately."

He smiled. "You think I'm clever. Sweet of you to say it."

"Please." She rolled her eyes. "You've been keeping shit to yourself from the moment you started dealing with us. We've enjoyed listening to the bullshit you've been peddling, but it's getting old. We're getting very good at knowing when you're trying to slip a fast one past us."

Ivan nodded. "All this sounds fantastic, but securing enough of the Verts to take control of the wormhole will be damn near impossible. Even if we doubled the rate we're pushing forward, which I think we can all agree would be dangerous, considering we don't know what we're dealing with, it still wouldn't be fast enough. Besides, if I remember correctly, the terms for you to inherit this treasure of yours is for the entirety of the station to be cleared, right? The place is big enough that it would take years to do that. That's assuming the infestation keeps being aggressive and attacking us. If it goes into hiding, it would take a lot longer to scan every section on the Serpent with a force ten times the size of what we've got now."

Kuzratha nodded. "Indeed. Using conventional means, it could very well take years to clear the station. However, I believe we could employ an unconventional tactic that would help us clear it a great deal faster."

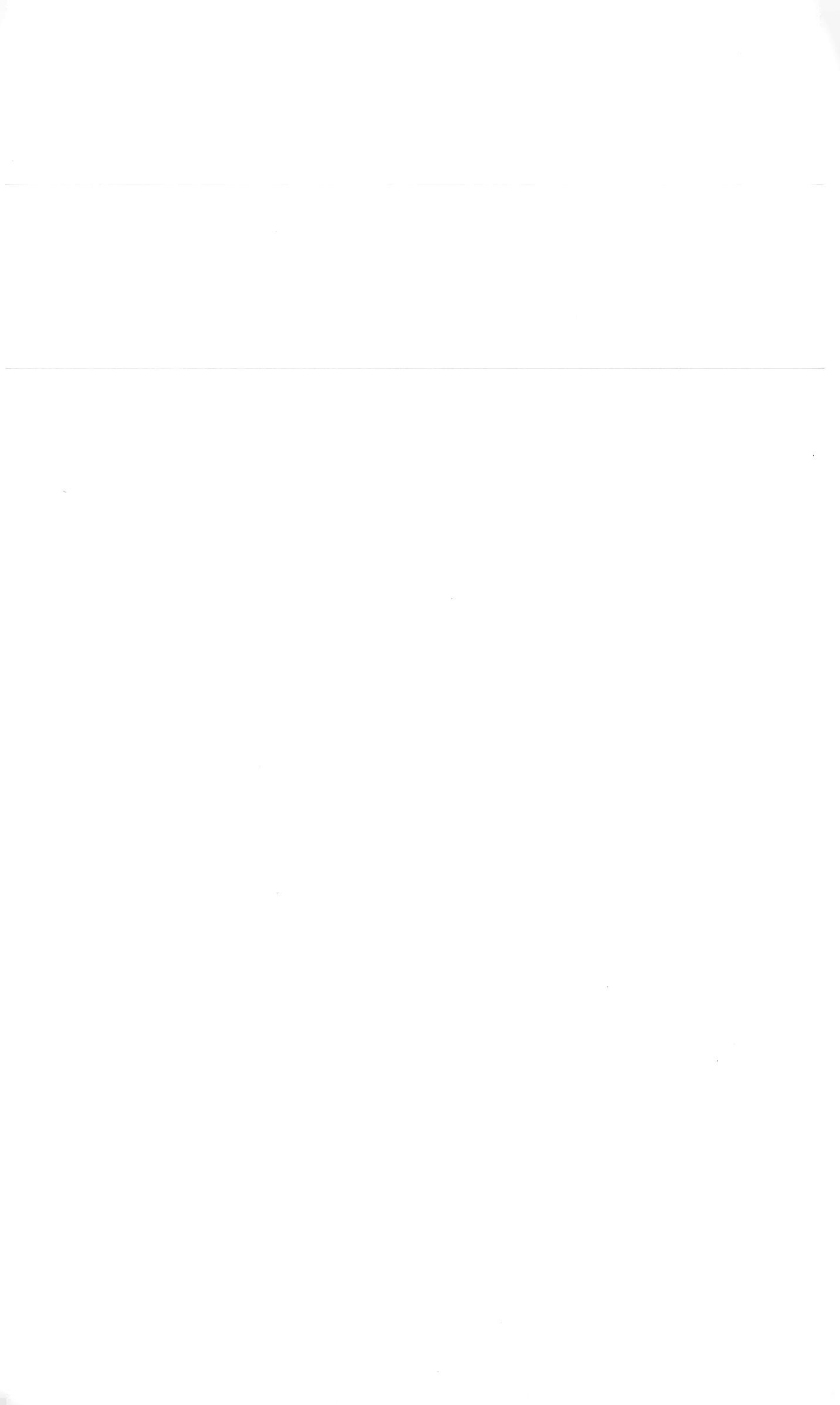

CHAPTER FIVE

Chill scowled. She was having a hard time believing what the Dahin was saying. She wanted to find a solution to the problem that had been vexing them for the past week. She also wanted to make sure they weren't going to be looking at the business end of a caster the moment the fighting stopped. There was no telling what the Over-Keeper would do to fuck them.

Trusting him wasn't an option. Still, if he was in a sharing mood, they could hear him out. If they didn't like it, they could tell him they would consider a change in plans. After they were back on the ship, she could bring up leaving.

It wouldn't be the first time they had done it, and she doubted it would be the last. After they were out of Jindahin space, they could share why they left with the rest of the galaxy and let the chips fall where they would. They would be blackballed by the corps, but if it got too bad, they could change their identities.

It wasn't the best solution, but she'd done it before, and

it had eventually worked out. It hadn't even been difficult. Since she had the required programming, it would be even easier after she adapted it to the upgraded security. That assumed it *had* been upgraded, which it had not been the last time she had erased shit about herself.

"All right." She nodded. "Let's hear what you've got in mind."

Kuzratha settled into his seat. "As the commander of the Janissaries told you, they are suspicious that there are tiers to the savages we've been facing."

Chill didn't point out that *he* hadn't faced anyone or anything. They would have to keep their mouths shut to find out what they were facing. That meant not contesting what he said.

"His suspicions are correct." He tilted his head. "Half-correct, anyway. The Treasure Keeper gave me access to the logs Lugosh kept while he was on the station. I was surprised to find that the tales of Lugosh leaving the Serpent after depositing his treasure here were intentional obfuscations."

"So, he died here?" Kortez asked, raising an eyebrow. "Doesn't change much."

"Let the Dahin say his piece," Chill urged, motioning for Kortez to keep his thoughts to himself for the moment. She wasn't sure if he understood why, but he nodded and gave her a thumbs-up.

"Thank you." Kuzratha returned his attention to the screen in front of him. "It would be best for you to see them yourselves." He projected the screen on a nearby wall to allow them to see the logs.

The Dahin on the screen was dressed in the finery

they'd come to expect from a space captain, although the look he was sporting was antiquated. He was taller and more powerful-looking than most of his species and had a commanding presence, although he was not as massive as the Janissaries.

Chill approached the screen. "That is Lugosh?"

"Indeed," the Treasure Keeper replied. "He secured his logs to keep the rest of his crew from seeing them. They can only be released to someone with biological markers from his family tree."

Lugosh was talking into a recording device in a language Chill didn't understand. It sounded like the traditional Jindahin dialect from the days before they had started teaching their children Galactic Common. Chill could understand a word here or there, but it was mostly gibberish.

"I've been working on a translation suite so more people can understand." The Over-Keeper tilted his head. "Mostly because my knowledge of the Old Tongue is rusty. They taught it to us during our instructional years, but there's so little use for it in the modern galaxy that most people only remember the basics. Anyway, here we go."

The recording rewound to the beginning. Lugosh began to record his log on a very old device.

"Captain Lugosh's log, date seventy-three, eighty-four, Mahlesh Ohkani. Blessings be. The station has been suffering from a lack of development, and after some convincing, the locals decided it would be best to hand over the controls to my crew and me. Thankfully, none of them had to die since we need most of the deckies to keep the station running. The Serpent is a fantastic place to defend against the Salifate junkies. We can also rebuild

our riches, our forces, and our situation from a position of strength here.

"It would take more than the forces they committed to the fight the last time to take this station, yet they left it undefended. That's one of the reasons I left the Salifate. They ignored our warnings about the weaknesses that would be exploited by those who opposed their mighty empire. I warned them of the Serpent's possibilities, but did they listen? No, they stripped me of my command and tried to have me indicted for treason."

"There's something the Jindahin probably wiped out of their history books," Chill muttered. The asshole might not be telling the truth, but these were his personal logs. There were plenty of reasons people lied to themselves, but it made sense that he would not do so here.

"That was early on," Kuzratha explained as the log advanced to the next message. "His plan was to set the Serpent up as a base so he could raid the planets inside the nebula. You'll see in a moment."

Lugosh continued, *"The riches on the planets inside the nebula were greatly exaggerated. There are substantial raw goods inside, but the planets will require decades to develop now that they have been colonized. It's not worth our time and effort. The Serpent itself is the prize we were all looking for. Vast amounts of power are lost to the inefficiencies of the station, and with some help from the treasures I brought on board, I believe I can bring it under my control."*

"There are more like that," Kuzratha muttered as he called up more logs. "Mostly talking about the state of the crew and their exploration of the station. Most of the settlers on the station had lost faith in the Jindahin leadership since they were suffering pirate attacks from every angle, so having a pirate show up to defend them seemed like a deal. Not all, though, as you'll see."

Another log came up. The Dahin looked frustrated.

"Our efforts to incorporate the dissidents into the station's operations have gone awry," he stated, a storm brewing in his eyes. *"Three of them attempted to take down the station's defenses and send a message to the Salifate command. They were intercepted, thanks to the AI I've installed, but I had to teach the group a lesson.*

"They were executed publicly, using biological agents from my vault. That should stop the rest of them. Our incinerators were damaged, so after some korring *and* kaing, *we decided to space them. It was not a popular decision, but we decided they would be better off in space than waiting to be cremated."*

"*Korring* and *kaing*?" Kortez asked, raising an eyebrow.

"Failure in the translation," Chill informed him. "Basically, a lot of conversation going back and forth between the two parties, if I remember correctly."

"You do," the AI answered.

"Oh, I think I see where this is going," Ivan whispered as the logs were fast-forwarded. "Hindsight being what it is. Can you send copies of those recordings to our ship so I can inspect them further?"

The Over-Keeper glared at him for a few seconds before nodding. "Naturally. But wait. Here comes the good part."

He apparently had a very different idea of what "the good part" meant, but she could see the pale blue markings moving across Lugosh's face in the recording the Over-Keeper showed them.

"The spiderwebbing in my veins is more worrying than the

doctors originally thought," Lugosh announced. *"They aren't sure what it is doing, but they assume I was exposed to the biological agent I applied to those rebellious assholes. They did say that it's not affecting my body's performance. I feel healthier than I did before. My blood pressure is lower, and I have better cardiovascular health overall. In the spirit of testing that, I repeated some training sims and noted a ten percent increase over my previous performances. If I've been infected, I'm not sure why those other assholes died from it. I've never felt better."*

Chill frowned. That was an odd type of biological agent. She didn't know how those worked, but they weren't supposed to kill all of those affected. Not the best ones, anyway. Those were supposed to infect a limited number of carriers who would pass the sickness along to the portion of the population that was not affected by the original attack.

Lugosh had that kind of knowledge, which meant there was something else going on in his head. It might indicate that his mental state had been affected by the biological agent.

In the next vid, he exhibited more physical symptoms. Maybe he was not a carrier, or not one who would be surviving for long.

"More infections have appeared on the station," he growled, breathing heavily. "Mostly in the Dahin and the humans, but among the other species as well. It's been working faster on the others, though. I'm not sure how, but they could have been infected for longer than me and just started showing symptoms.

"Three-quarters of those infected die quickly. The others show the same symptoms as me, but they are progressing quicker. Residents report sightings of those who died of the infection as well,

although most started showing symptoms immediately afterward, so their word is suspect.

"So is mine, as it turns out. I have seen creepers as well, looking dead but very much alive, out of the corner of my eye. Am I going mad? I will continue to document my case as the symptoms continue. Hopefully, it will help those who are developing a cure."

Chill was silent as the log advanced to the next message. It was not a pleasant sight to see someone dying slowly and painfully. The Dahin was covering it, maybe trying to convince himself he wasn't in pain, but it was obvious. Chronic agony could not be hidden for long.

It was not working out the way he had wanted it to, but Chill could see the hallmarks of an arrogant man who would not give in, no matter how many people were pushing him to make the changes that would save his life.

She crossed her arms as the next vid was projected. Now his eyes were showing signs of infection. He was speaking, but the translator was having a hard time keeping up with what he was saying.

Fewer of the words were familiar. Some were slurred, and most were spoken in a jumble that even an AI familiar with the language couldn't process.

"There are a few more of these," Kuzratha said, calling them up. "Just him mumbling and babbling. Sometimes what he's saying is apparent, but most of the time, he's just showing how far he's gone."

Lugosh repeated some of the unintelligible words, but she still couldn't understand them. He seemed to forget there was a recorder trained on him too. He babbled to items on his desk but paused to take calls from elsewhere on the station. On those, he spoke normally. After those conversations were over, he reverted to mumbling.

"It's hard to watch such a great mind, one of the greatest in our military's history, slipping," the Over-Keeper whispered."

"He's not slipping," Kortez interjected. "He's still giving orders, just not the kind we can understand."

Chill turned to her crewmate. "What are you talking about?"

"Haven't you been paying attention?" The larger man chuckled, shook his head, and pulled up several of their recordings from the recent attacks. "Those groans and growls from the creepers? Most are just what's louder than the rest, but when I was sitting with Dorian, looking at the footage, he enhanced the audio we collected. Said he'd been doing it since the Bugz, when he wanted to figure out what they were saying without speaking. Called it up, and sure enough..."

His voice trailed off as he played bits where they could hear sounds similar to what Lugosh was saying to his recorder. Not the same, but they were familiar.

Chill grunted. "How the hell could a biological weapon cause the infected to develop a new language and speech patterns?"

"Beats me, but whatever he put out there isn't anything like we've ever seen. It's possible it wasn't even a weapon. Might have been a terraforming agent."

That was an interesting way of looking at it. Not that she bought the idea, but it was a possibility. Terraforming agents were expensive, costing trillions of creds to develop and worth even more to the corps who wanted more planets. If Lugosh had stumbled on a lab that created those, it was possible he didn't know what he'd picked up.

"Does it keep going like this, or does he eventually start making sense again?" Chill asked. She'd realized that they weren't resolving anything.

"Oh, yes." Kuzratha cleared his throat as he forwarded through dozens of entries. "Later events cause him to regain his focus, although it doesn't last for long."

Chill made a mental note to give Alex the logs. Their AI could possibly run algorithms that would allow them to understand what the creepers were saying to each other. That would give them an advantage the Scourge apparently never thought to use.

Finally, they got to a log where Lugosh was focused. He stared into the recorder as he had on the earlier vids.

"Resources are dwindling." His eyes narrowed, and his fingers clenched on the table. He was fighting to focus on what he was saying. "Hard... I don't know. The infection is taking over the station. Deckies are being forced out of the control sections of the Serpent, although it doesn't look like it's causing any structural damage.

"We've held strong here at the central control station, but I'm not sure how...how long it'll last. Deckies are fighting now too. Think...I'm responsible for the outbreak. They forgot I was the one who got the pirates off their backs!"

Lugosh transitioned from calm and rational to foaming at the mouth in less than a second, pounding his fist on the table and knocking his recorder over. He took a few seconds to set it back up.

"I'm having my AI use the station's defenses to fight the infection. The Scourge program should slow the infection down

long enough for them to develop a cure. Still months away, they say, but I think I can hold it off for that long. I have to."

The recording cut off abruptly, leaving Chill staring at the next segment.

"'*I think I can hold it off for that long,*'" she repeated. "You think he was talking about the infection on the rest of the station or in him?"

"Either," Ivan suggested. "Both. Him thinking he could will himself to stay healthy against a biological agent ravaging his body seems about right. Could also be a sign of the shit turning his brain to mush."

That was the likelier option. He was losing it, yet somehow keeping himself from being further infected. As the leader, he would have access to medical options the rest of the station didn't. It could also explain why he was fighting the infection more effectively than the rest of them.

However, there was no sign of it having stopped and no cure. She knew how the logs would end. If he'd recovered, they would know. There would have been indications. More importantly, he would have found a way to eradicate the infection from the rest of the station. Then they would have heard stories about the dread pirate Lugosh, based on the Serpent, terrorizing the rest of the galaxy.

The next recording came up. His face was covered with spiderwebbed veins. Once again, what they were looking at was familiar but different from what they had seen in the creepers so far.

Maybe that was what the commanders of the creepers looked like.

"They... Fuckers!" He hit the table again, and knocked the

recorder over. This time, he didn't bother to set it up. *"They think they can...they can run the fucking station better than I can? Kill them all! Kill all the fucking shits! I'll kill them* all!"

His speech went back to the grumbling and growling of the creepers. It sounded like he was sending out orders to the creatures in the vicinity, although there was no response.

"They found a cure. Or they say it's a cure, the little shits. It's just a way to kill all the creepers. They say it's our only chance to salvage the station, but I know. I know! It's just a way to kill me so they can take control! I know!"

Kuzratha paused the recording and looked around with a twinkle in his eye. "See there? A cure, or at the very least, a way to cleanse the whole station in one fell swoop."

"We can only hope," Chill answered. "That's not what he's saying. Best to keep watching."

The Over-Keeper rolled his eyes. "Of course it's not what he's saying. He was gone by this point if he saw an attempt by his people to cleanse the station as a coup. Here, keep watching."

That had been her suggestion, but Chill didn't remind him.

Lugosh continued ranting, jumping from the creeper language to the other one.

"They took it from my blood, the bastards. Called it the 'alpha infection.' Said they needed samples, but they're just looking for a way to kill me. They won't kill me... Won't fucking..."

The recording ended, and the next one showed him looking more composed and in control of himself.

"The rebellion was quelled," he stated. He stared into the recorder, his near-black eyes making Chill uncomfortable.

"They will not be using the cure as long as I am still in control of my body. Even if it were to purge my body of the infection, I would have to live in a sealed environment for the rest of my life, which they are telling me would be considerably longer than most Dahin live. The infection is extending my life, it seems. I don't understand how that is possible, but I will take their word for it."

He was fighting. His body was so tense that he trembled, and he was clenching his fists to keep his hands under control. It was one of his few moments of lucidity, but he wasn't going to stay in that state for long.

"I cannot fight the Creeper's Call for much longer," he continued, his voice cracking. *"I will abdicate my command, and I have sealed what remains of my treasure in a place where only I can reach it as an incentive to those still working on a cure to find one that will affect me.*

"If they are not successful, another member of my family can open the vault once the creepers can't taint it. Those who remained loyal among my cadre will continue finding the cure, and when the time is right, they will administer it to me. They will find a way. I know it."

It was the last recording. Given the date, it had gone unseen for six decades.

"I'm going to guess that Lugosh's faith in his crew was misplaced," Chill stated to break the silence that had fallen over their group.

"You are correct," the AI answered with a smile. "Without Lugosh's magnetic presence to guide them, his crew succumbed to infighting. One of the factions eventually tainted my coding of the Scourge, sending those they controlled to attack the others. They were successful, but they failed to understand the adaptive properties of the

Scourge and so didn't anticipate that the bots they had sicced on their comrades would turn on them as well. The last member of Lugosh's crew perished six months after he abdicated command. The others had died months before that."

"Still, there is reason to hope," Kuzratha interrupted. "With the Treasure Keeper's help, I recovered part of the formula developed to kill the creepers. However, we are missing a few key components. I believe this to be what they found in Lugosh's alpha strain.

"If my assumptions are right and there *are* commanders out there, they might have the alpha strain in their blood, and we could use it. Lugosh might still be alive among the creepers, drawn by the Call to join their barbaric communities."

"You really think the old bastard is still alive and well?" Kortez asked.

"You heard him. The infection was prolonging his life to well beyond what could be expected from the average Dahin. If that is true, he might still be alive among the beasts."

"If that's true—and that's a massive if—what do you suggest we do about it?" Chill raised an eyebrow. "You said it yourself; we're on a clock."

"We can set a trap for one of the commanders. Perhaps even Lugosh," Kuzratha suggested. "Then we can collect a sample of the alpha strain, and from there, we can develop the creeper-killing reagent and use it in the air scrubbers to cleanse the station."

CHAPTER SIX

"You really think we can pull it off?" Kortez spoke to her as she cleaned out her suit and prepared it for future attacks.

She shrugged. "I'm not sure I'm willing to commit to the plan one way or the other. It reeks of the Over-Keeper's desperation to keep control of the station. He might be looking to continue his ancestor's dream of controlling the Serpent without Dahin Authority looking over his shoulder."

"I don't know. There might be something to it," Ivan commented. "If there *is* a central command for the creepers, they would be the ones to get a sample from if we're going to make an antidote."

"It's not like any of us has the ability to come up with a cure," Chill reminded them. "The best we can hope for is that an ages-old AI can pull it off with what limited facilities it still has. Then we have to hope the infestation will react to the reagent we come up with. It's a long shot at best and one I'm not sure I want to commit my people to."

She knew she shouldn't have said that. It should have

waited until she had a better idea of what their mindset was.

Ivan turned to face her.

"You got something on your mind, boss?" he asked. Chill realized that not only was Kortez listening too, but Zichix was also tuned in as he climbed down from one of the vents into the loading bay.

Hell, Dorian was probably listening to the conversation from the cockpit.

Chill nodded and took a deep breath before answering.

"I think we've done all we can do on this station." She nodded, committing herself to what she had been thinking for a long time. "I doubt the Over-Keeper will let us just walk away, but we should probably let the deckies know what they're up against and offer them the chance to leave before this place is turned to scrap by the Jindahin navy. That's what I think we should do."

She paused and looked at the trio. Kortez and Ivan were nodding.

"Yeah, I know that's not what we signed on for. It's not what we're known for either, and it sure as fuck isn't the kind of mentality that got us this far. However, we didn't sign on for killer robots *not* being the most terrifying thing to come at us on this station."

She felt cowardly for thinking it, and saying that out loud didn't help matters. The DEMC generally stuck it out no matter how tough things got. If they had any chance to win, they pushed for it.

They'd survived so far, but they were all looking to her for direction. Chill had to be the voice of reason, whether she wanted to or not, before they went further down this path and got killed.

"Is that really what you think we should do?" Kortez asked.

"I don't know." Chill sighed, put her tools down, and rubbed her eyes, although her hands were covered with grease. "We always charge into the mouth of crazy and headbutt it until it gives up or we've smashed it to pieces. This time, we need to consider the options. Walking away from this situation, which is bigger than all of us, might be the best choice."

"I'm not sure it is," Zichix pointed out. "I don't really know how these situations work, but what I've seen of human behavior leads me to believe that walking away from one fight will turn into you walking away from another and another. It'll wreck your confidence and the confidence others have in you."

"Better than ending up dead," Kortez pointed out. "I doubt we're going to walk away from this fight, but Chill is right. We need to consider the alternative."

"Let's consider it," Ivan answered. "We have a couple of weeks to consider it. It's not a decision any of us wants to make on the spur of the moment. Headbutting monsters until they break? That's a spur-of-the-moment decision. Everything else should probably be slept on."

"That's reasonable," Chill agreed. That wasn't a word she would ascribe to her or any of the crew, but they were parents now. Well, Kortez was, which meant they had to think about the best course of action rather than jumping in.

She wondered if she *was* a coward, wanting to save her

own life in the face of odds that she could escape but others couldn't.

It wouldn't have been the first time she had run from trouble. She'd done it before, and Zichix was right about one thing; it had destroyed her confidence. She'd been running from her past for years. She doubted she would ever stop running.

"So, we're putting the topic aside for now." Zichix nodded, or rather, moved his eyestalks up and down to imitate a human nod. "Can we talk about the Janissaries?"

"What about them?" Chill asked, picking her tools up and returning her attention to her suit.

"You know they ran a sweep of the ship when we docked, right?"

"Sure."

"There's just something about their presence that unsettles the ship. Makes her feel different for a few hours after they've left. Every time."

She studied their surroundings, wondering if there was something to what he was talking about.

"I...yeah… There's... Sorry, I'm not picking up on anything."

"Don't worry about it. I've come to terms with having finer senses than you humans." He smiled at her with his eyes. "Still, there is something different about the ship. Something she hasn't shaken off yet. Like, it's...clinging. I don't know."

She wondered if it had something to do with the genetic manipulation that had created the Janissaries. They were different, that much was obvious, but if those changes left a distinct impression beings like Zichix could pick up on, the science might have gone too far.

"All right," Dorian announced over the intercom. "We're cleared for departure. Should get back to Coil Cove in under an hour."

"You need me up there?" Chill asked as Ibu closed her suit and walked it to its harness. Ivan and Kortez followed her.

"The turrets we'll encounter were either commandeered or melted, so I can handle it," Dorian told her. "Just sit back and enjoy the ride."

Chill chuckled. The ride wouldn't be enjoyable. If they had any downtime, she wanted to give Alex the recordings they'd gotten from the Over-Keeper. She didn't have high hopes for the AI finding anything useful, but it couldn't hurt.

"Something's wrong," Zichix insisted, his eyes moving independently of each other as he scanned the loading bay.

"Those fucking Janissaries can't just leave anything to us," Kortez muttered. "The kid's worried, so I'm not going to get a wink of sleep."

"Oh, Dad," Zichix answered. "I can move my anxiety to another room if you need to sleep."

"Nah. I'll just be thinking about you being anxious. Best to sort this out now, regardless of how long it takes."

"Thanks, Dad. You're the best e—"

Zichix stopped talking. Chill turned away from working on her suit's software to find out what was wrong. His eyestalks weren't moving anymore. They were focused on something near the vents he used to travel through the ship. They were avenues only he could use, so it reduced the possibility of someone accidentally treading on his legs.

It happened more often than she would have liked. While the kid was a good sport about it, she could understand him wanting an easy way to traverse the ship.

But that wasn't what he was looking at. His limbs were trembling, and he was drawing back. Chill was not an expert, but his body language was shouting that he was terrified of something he could see but the rest of the team couldn't.

Then they could. She tried to identify whatever was moving across the overhead as she reached for the knife that was not there, being attached to her suit. Then she heard the low, dull groaning of the creepers' communications.

"Zichix, move!"

Her warning didn't come in time. The creature noticed that Zichix could see it and it was on him in the blink of an eye. She heard a screech of pain from Zichix as she and Kortez dove in to help.

The creeper was stringy, with no right to be as strong as it was. It took her, Kortez, and Ivan to drag it clear of Zichix and pin it to the deck. Ivan hacked at the head until it stopped fighting to get back to Zichix.

"There are more of them," Chill announced. "Dorian, seal the cockpit!"

"What?" he asked over the intercom.

"No time! Seal the cockpit now! Emergency protocols!"

He did as he was told. Kortez and Ivan tended to Zichix, who had shallow wounds on his abdomen from the jagged knife the dead creeper had wielded. His abdomen was thin, which meant those gashes could have easily hit something vital.

"How's he doing?" Chill asked as she went back to the suits.

"I'll be fine," Zichix answered, sounding shaky. "It didn't hit anything vital, and I closed off my sections to keep the blood loss down. There are more of them, and they are the threat you need to pay attention to."

"If you think I'm going to leave you behind, you lost more blood than you think, little guy," Kortez growled. He picked Zichix up and helped him wrap around his dad's body.

"Yeah, you guys are going to want to look around the ship," Dorian called. "I'm picking up movement and life signs that shouldn't be there all over the fucking place."

"Why didn't you pick up on them before?" Chill growled.

"I don't know. The fucking creepers can hide from the usual scans? Maybe I didn't check for extra life signs as thoroughly as I should have, but are we really playing the blame game now?"

"No, but we're going to play it later," Kortez snarled.

"How many signs?" Chill asked to change the subject. They didn't have the time to get their suits up and running. Ibu could do that without help. Chill took her knife and the hammer off her suit.

"It's hard to say, but they're all over the fucking ship. How did they get here?"

She had no answers. Chill saw the signals he was talking about popping up all over the place.

"We're going to retake the ship. Start with the controls.

Outside the cockpit, it's the only spot where they could end up killing us all with the press of a button. Let's get moving."

It occurred to her that saying that out loud was a bad idea. They didn't have any idea where the creatures were or what kind of tech they understood, so identifying their targets for them was a bad idea. Kortez carried Cortador, and Ivan had his knives to work with.

She thought they could handle a small pack of the creepers without their suits. Whether they could do so and leave their ship intact? The redundancies would help them, but they weren't far from the vacuum of space. One wire yanked, one button pressed, and they would be sucking on nothing for the rest of their very short lives.

It did beg the question of why they were only attacking now. Was it because they had just been spotted? Had they been too terrified to attack before? It didn't seem like they had any self-preservation instincts, but if there was ever a time to keep from being found, it was when the ship was being searched by the Janissaries. Maybe the Dahin had had the same "off" feeling Zichix had expressed. The creepers apparently knew to stay low and hard to find when the big warriors were around.

Those were questions for later. They should get professionals in to autopsy one of the critters they'd killed. That might get them infected, though.

That was another issue for her to bring up in the near future. The source had been easily transmissible at one point. Were they already infected, or did certain conditions have to be present before that happened?

Her heart was hammering, and her thoughts were

jumbled, although she didn't want to blame the possible infection for that yet.

A low groan warned her of an attack a second before one of the creatures came out of the shadows and lunged for her as she reached the control room. Her raised blade deflected something jagged and sharp aimed for her chest. The hammer in her right hand whined as she brought it around to crush it into the creeper's skull. Blood and tissue splattered the walls. She saw a pair of Ivan's knives jutting from its chest after it hit the deck.

"You think we should, like, clean that shit up?" Kortez asked. "Are we in danger of being infected by it?"

"The greater danger is getting gutted by those shits," Chill growled, kicking the improvised knife out of the hands of the creeper she'd taken out. "After we're clear of that danger, we will find out if there are other problems to deal with."

Kortez nodded and patted Zichix. The alien was wrapped around him tighter than usual, but that was to be expected. He was hurting, and he needed his dad.

Having casters would have been nice, but they kept those in the cockpit. She hoped Dorian had armed up, though he probably didn't want to join the fighting. She was fine with that as long as he sealed the cockpit against intruders. It was small enough that with the doors and vents closed, the creepers could not sneak in without him noticing. If they did, he would take them out.

She had to focus; Dorian was safer than they were right now. The scanners told her two creepers were inside the control room. Chill motioned for Ivan to go in first and Kortez to bring up the rear. They had the drop on the creatures, and they were going to take advantage of it.

Ivan stepped in, and the pair of knives he launched on entry caught his targets in the throats. They didn't have the same damage points as humans or the Scourge bots. The knives in their necks did cause damage, but they were far from out of the fight.

Chill came in behind him and dropped to one knee. She dodged a lunging thrust at her head as she slammed her hammer through the legs of the first creature. Ivan had pinned the second one to the deck, and Kortez bellowed one of his battle cries as he hacked its head off.

Quick, smooth, professional. Just the way they'd been taught to do it. The one Chill took down was still alive, groaning and grasping for whatever it could reach before Kortez chopped its head off too.

"Was that necessary?" Ivan asked, raising an eyebrow.

"I believe it was."

"Not the time," Chill hissed. "Kortez, you and Zichix are going to seal yourselves in here and make sure those two didn't cause any damage. Ivan and I are going to keep sweeping the ship."

That would keep Zichix away from the fighting, and from Kortez's nod, he understood that.

"All right, we're out of here." Chill flicked dark blood off her blade. "Don't open anything until you get the all-clear, understood?"

"We got this," Zichix chirped.

CHAPTER SEVEN

The scanners were not telling them where the life signs were coming from. The creepers could apparently keep themselves from being spotted.

Chill thought it was because they were dead, or at least not alive in the way they had been before the infection. Sensors looked for the electrical impulses associated with heartbeats or synaptic impulses, which worked even for those beings who didn't have a standard cardiovascular system.

Those markers were hard to detect but distinctive, so the sensors had to be set to the highest sensitivity. They could pick up those pulses from large distances, no matter how much interference there was.

The creepers could switch theirs off, or possibly, they weren't active and therefore had no synaptic presence until they got orders, for lack of a better term. That was the only plausible explanation for why they kept showing up and disappearing on the sensors. If they were getting orders, where were they coming from? How were they reaching the creepers without being detected?

No, it had to be an internal solution. Even though they were made up of biological materials, they could switch themselves on and off the way bots did. That kept them from being spotted while they were dormant.

Chill took a deep breath and tapped a panel.

"Venting doing its thing?" Ivan asked. He had his knives in hand and was keeping a watchful eye out for approaching creatures.

"Loading bay and outer rooms had their atmo vented, but we can't do that in the central parts of the ship. Still, it narrows our search. Those bastards are hiding and angling around to attack from behind, which is really fucking annoying."

She was stating the obvious. Ivan replied, "You have to admit it's interesting to see how they work."

Chill didn't tell him that was stupid. Better to hear what he had to say, *then* subject him to mockery.

He realized she was waiting for him to explain. "They managed to get on the ship without anyone noticing until Zichix picked up on what they were doing. The creatures are not only smart enough to avoid engaging the Janissaries but also smart enough to attack us tactically. Fuck, if Zichix hadn't spotted them, we would have waltzed back to Coil Cove with a ship full of the bastards. We wouldn't have known we were under attack or being infected until they were right on top of us."

"What is your point?" Chill asked, annoyed. She didn't want to think about the ramifications of their situation.

If they had returned to Coil Cove with the creepers on

their ship, they would have been responsible for whatever happened. Either the crews would get infected, or they would all be killed, and it would be their fault.

More concerning was the revelation that they were dealing with an enemy who could plan their attacks. Also, that enemy could use the scraps of the people they killed, so the mercs could never eradicate them.

"No real point." Ivan smirked. "It just feels like we're up against a real army this time. If they're going to attack us like this, we should return the favor."

"We'll have to try to trap one of their commanders so we can try to develop an antidote."

He nodded. "It's not like we have an abundance of options."

Chill sighed. She couldn't think of another plan that would let them clear the station in less than the two weeks they apparently had. Even if they had a couple of years, she doubted they could accomplish that task with the resources at hand.

"All right, the loading bay is clear," Chill reported. "Rooms and storage areas too. The control room and the cockpit are both clear. We have to clear the hallways, and it looks like there are plenty there. I'll run point if you'll pick them off from a distance."

"Just avoid the flying knives."

They could open the doors to get more support, but Ibu had climbed into one of the suits while the atmo was vented from the loading bay, and Kortez and Zichix were covering the control room. Dorian was holding the cockpit, so they had control of the ship. They wouldn't dock in Coil Cove until it was clear.

Dorian had sent word that their ship had been compromised and they were holding their position.

They were ready. Their enemies were contained, their weapons primed. They could attack. The creepers' signals were still flickering and jumping around, making it difficult to pin down where they were, but there were at least twelve. They were hugging the walls, so Chill couldn't engage in the kind of fighting she liked.

If they had to hack their way through the creatures, Ivan would take them out while she drove in. It would mean acquiring cuts and bruises, and she wasn't happy about doing it without her armor, but better her than him.

"All right, let's get moving." She turned the hammer on, grabbed a knife, and took a deep breath to settle her nerves before opening the door.

The corridor was the optimal place for the coming fight. It narrowed the creepers' avenues of attack so they could not overwhelm their defenses.

"Come out, come out, wherever you are!" Chill called, twirling her hammer to build momentum for the inertia generator. As she ducked to the right to begin her charge, a cut on her cheek told her she'd missed a creeper. She didn't realize she had swung her blade until she slashed the intruder's throat to the spine.

Even with its head dangling by a thread of tissue, the body kept attacking until she severed the head. She slammed her whining hammer into a second creeper's shoulder. It collapsed in a twitching pile of blood and viscera as Chill pressed forward.

The two behind it each had knives in their chests. They were yanked forward as Ivan called his knives back to him.

He dragged them into the paths of Chill's knife and hammer, and she finished the take-downs.

Neither was destroyed, but she kicked them out of the way and looked for the next target. Ivan could finish them off at his leisure.

The creeper behind them had several gaping chest wounds. Its right arm had been rendered useless, but it was carrying a chunk of metal she hoped hadn't come from their ship. The creeper swung it wildly, but Chill side-stepped the attack, then hacked the arm off. Another pair of creepers tried to use it as a shield, but she rushed forward and slammed her hammer into the head of the one approaching from her right side.

The inertial generator had enough power to carry the hammer into the next one, crushing its head into the wall and splattering everything inside onto the walls and deck.

Chill wasn't sure how they could clean and disinfect the 'vette so they didn't carry the infection back. The process would require help from the deckies. She would have Alex scan the ship for foreign substances.

They had the tech to prevent them from strewing dangerous foreign particles about the galaxy. They just had to scrub the damn ship.

Ivan held the few creepers who remained against the door of the cockpit. His knives pinned them in place for Chill to finish off.

Chill ensured there was nothing useful for them to recover, though it added to the cleaning burden. Their groans died when their throats collapsed.

"Tearing these creepers apart is a lot more satisfying

than wrecking Scourge bots." Chill carefully cleaned the dark blood off her knife and her hammer.

"Is everything okay?" Dorian asked over the intercom. "You guys all alive?"

"Yes," Ivan replied. "But we made a mess. You'll want to stay in the cockpit until everything's been sterilized."

"Oh, no problem there. I just wanted to make sure you were all still alive." Dorian paused. "I'll bring us into the Cove. There will be a lot of time for us to regale each other with the battle stories we accumulated."

"'We accumulated?'" Chill repeated, raising an eyebrow. "That was an impressive bit of sitting you did in the cockpit."

Dorian gasped. "How dare you? I was worried sick for your well-being in here, ready to give my life by scuttling the ship so the infection didn't spread to our comrades."

"Bullshit. You were in there playing Kang the Explorer while we were fighting dozens of monsters," Chill shot back, shaking her head. "But on to something vital to our situation. Have you scanned the ship? We need to make sure there aren't any more creepers before we land in Coil Cove."

"It was Kontar the Conqueror," Dorian corrected. "The far superior sequel. And there's nothing more on the ship for us to deal with. Still, nothing's going to convince me our ship is clear of the bastards until we send it into the nebula and wreck it."

"Only if you're going to fly it."

"We could always trade it to someone."

Chill smirked. The soft creaking of the hull told her they had entered the Cove. "If you think *you're* paranoid about the creatures, can you imagine how everyone else on the station is going to feel? Unless you plan on scuttling the ship and stranding us on a station full of the bastards until someone can offer us a lift, I suggest we just clear the ship and hope our sensors are working this time."

"You sure know how to fill me with confidence."

"Just returning the favor, kid."

Dorian had the automated systems purge the interior with radiation that killed viruses and bacteria, as well as small life forms. Some arachnid and insectoid species could not only survive under heavy loads of radiation but thrive. Other protocols were required to purge them from ships that might transport them to planets with no natural predators. Only once every nook and cranny had been cleared out did they open the other compartments.

Kortez had tended Zichix's wounds. While they didn't look serious, Chill remembered that his ability to move was based on a system similar to the hydraulics that powered their suits. Any breach in the pressurization of his exoskeleton meant he would have a hard time walking, much less moving fast if needed.

Chill would never forgive the fucking creepers injuring him, but she suspected her rage paled in comparison to Kortez's.

When she got to the loading bay, Ibu was still in a suit. She'd picked a couple of the creepers off before she vented the room. All that was left was the smell of charred meat and black splotches around the suit.

"Have fun down here?" Chill asked, raising an eyebrow.

"Only three of them. It was more target practice," Ibu answered.

"You coming out of the suit?"

"Not for a bit. Still got the jitters, and I'll feel better with a couple tons of armor between me and anything that might try to kill me."

"Fair enough. Let me know if I can get you anything."

Shoviil greeted them as they came off the ship, looking concerned. He was flanked by a dozen armed deckies ready for a fight.

"You're all alive!" He sighed. "Good. We thought…well, given your communication that your ship had been breached, we thought you weren't going to make it. Is everyone all right?"

Chill nodded. "Zichix took some damage, but I think he'll live. We're keeping an eye on him."

"What about you?"

"What about me?"

Shoviil studied her like he wasn't sure how to answer, which forced her to question her situation until she saw her face on a nearby surface.

In the adrenaline-fueled action, she'd missed the damage she'd taken. Her shoulders were scratched and covered in dried blood. Her cheeks had smears of it as well, although none of it touched her new silver scar. Her hair was matted with blood too.

It wasn't her best look, but not her worst either. She looked worse when she woke up. Still, when it was pointed out to her, she suddenly felt the damage she'd taken. The painful, itchy cuts probably needed attention from their onboard physician —if *he* wasn't in desperate need of medical attention.

She could take care of it herself, although she would

have to raid a few of Zichix's stores of antibiotics and antivirals to make sure she didn't catch anything from the cuts.

"I'll be fine." Having amended her previous statement, Chill continued. "We have news about how we're going to be dealing with the creepers from this point forward. Kuzratha's research says we can get all the fucking creepers out of the way in one fell swoop, but it's going to require a lot of cooperation between the crews."

"I understand. I'll start gathering the leaders of the merc and decky crews so we can put a plan in place." Shoviil turned, already keying into his comm.

"What are we going to tell them?" Kortez asked. Zichix was still wrapped around him, but the wounds had all been sealed to avoid the risk of external bacteria or viruses making their way in.

"What do you mean?"

"Well, we have a new timeline. We can say Kuzratha changed the timeline to two weeks and this is how we're going to do it, or we can tell them the Jindahin fleet is going to be here in two weeks, and we need to clear the station by then or risk having them kill us all."

Ivan tilted his head. "There are benefits to being truthful, but the mercs and the deckies would probably decide they didn't want to deal with that bullshit and leave. That wouldn't be terrible, but we need our fighting force to capture a creeper commander."

"If we cleared the creepers out with the reagent, our reward would increase," Kortez pointed out. "We would also have a lot less leverage to deal with the Jindahin, assuming they want to take over the station and don't want to pay the mercs who did the work."

"Truth is the better option," Chill decided. "Otherwise, we're risking running into the situation we had with the Hammers. When the Jindahin show up, the mercs will find out we kept shit from them. The deckies too, and after that, I doubt we could convince them we kept the situation a secret for *their* safety."

Kortez, Ivan, and Zichix were silent.

"I hate to say it, but she has a point," Ivan finally muttered. "We're already on shaky ground with the deckies and the mercs. Telling them is the best way to keep them on our side if something goes badly. Otherwise, they might assume we're in league with the Jindahin and kick us out."

"Yeah," Kortez agreed. "Dorian, what do you think?"

Dorian shrugged. "It seems like you have this under control. I'm more than happy to abide by whatever decision you make."

Chill sighed. "Still on that fucking game?"

"Kontar the Conqueror?" Ivan asked. "Way superior to the original. It's not often that they make the second game better than the first, but hitching it to the best sim engines in the business makes it a lot more immersive."

She blinked a few times. "You play it too?"

"Are you kidding? I'm the one who introduced Dorian to the series. It's one of the best sim combat tac shooters on the market. I've been following the dev company since they started out with Eartha, Hard Kills."

Shooters and tac simulators had never been her kind of games. She had building sims on her tablets to calm her.

They were fun and engaged her creativity while letting her mind wander.

But that wasn't what they were talking about.

"I think being honest is best, although we might get some resistance," she stated firmly. "If they decide to leave, they'll do it based on the big picture. If they stick around, they'll probably be rewarded for remaining."

Kortez nodded. "What happens if they all disappear? I mean, we can't pull this shit off on our own."

"We'll do our best," Chill answered. "If we have to clear more of the station on our own, we can demand a lot more money, as well as letting the Jindahin take over the station without anybody putting up a fight. Our reputation will take a hit, but if we're well-compensated for our work, we won't need to worry about that for a while."

They all nodded.

"We'll have to be ready for the bad reactions we'll get from the rest of the crews." Ivan scowled, nodding at the groups gathering around their ship. None seemed happy about being called in for the conversation, but if word had gotten out that they were looking at wiping all the creepers out for good, they would want to hear the plan.

"You're thinking of how Lugosh's team rebelled and forced him to give up control of his crew?" Kortez narrowed his eyes. "We can pull that off if you want to, but you keep saying you're not the captain, which takes the fun out of a mutiny."

"I suppose it does." Chill sighed. The bright side was that if the rest ran the DEMC off the station, they wouldn't have to decide what to do about staying. They could just let the chips fall where they may.

Shoviil came up the ramp to their ship. He stopped to check on Zichix before coming over to Chill. "The word that we're planning to clear all the fucking monsters off the station was enough to get everyone here, but they don't believe you can pull it off. I think that if anyone can do it, it's you guys."

Chill nodded. "We were and are skeptical too, yet we're going to give it a try. We have to make sure we're not leaving any proverbial stones unturned since there are other elements at play. The Over-Keeper told us some stuff, likely thinking we were going to keep it to ourselves, but we've learned that it is in everyone's best interests if we put all our cards on the table."

The Xo-Trang decided to let Chill have her say and then make a decision.

"This is probably as many people as we're going to get," Chill announced. Shoviil had set up a live link for the crews who couldn't make it. Many were in the field or prepping to go out, so they couldn't come.

She waved at the crowd to get their attention, then began, "We have a problem. The creepers and the infection they spread isn't the type of threat we are used to dealing with. A group of them just attacked our ship. If you see that as incompetence on our part, that's fine."

This was like the state addresses the corps broadcast from time to time. The crowd was listening, although several grumbled that they had better things to do.

"We now know that while Lugosh did leave his treasure on the Serpent, he didn't make it off the station. He accidentally unleashed the infection, as well as the Scourge, which was supposed to contain the infection. Then his people turned the Scourge on their enemies, which backfired in a colossal way. That's a whole other story."

She had their attention. The mumbling and grumbling stopped.

"The point is, a handful of the original infected individuals survived and appear to be commanding the creepers. What remained of Lugosh's crew tried to create a cure using what they called the 'alpha strain,' which Lugosh carried. We can develop a reagent if we capture one of the commanders and get a sample of that strain. Then we would put it in the station's atmo scrubbers and clean up the infestation.

"It won't be simple or easy to capture a commander, and the reagent might not be effective, but we're now under a time crunch, so our best option is to cleanse the station in the allotted two weeks."

That was a good segue into her next point, although it did get more grumbles and complaints from the crowd as well as those who were watching from afar.

"I'm sure you want to know about the new time crunch." Chill took a deep breath. Her stomach fluttered, which made it difficult to focus. "As you know, the Jindahin are sponsoring the effort to retake the station. Turns out they are not happy with the methodical approach we've been using.

"They gave us two weeks to finish our work—the time it will take them to get a fleet here. They haven't stated what comes next, but I personally assume we will all be pushed aside. If we resist, they will use force. If their push does not go to plan, they will probably blow up the station."

It was risky to include that last part, but they had to

know what was coming and why and what was likely to happen when the Jindahin arrived. Some might be thinking the Dahin weren't giving them a fair shot at the task, but she'd dealt with them before. She'd seen how they handled native species in areas they took over.

It wasn't pleasant.

"I...*we* wanted to let you know what was coming," she continued, looking at the crowd. "If you want to leave before the two-week mark, we understand. If so, pack your shit. We'll see about hiring merc ships to get those who wish to leave and don't have transportation to the nearest system. Then you'll be on your own.

"The DEMC will remain on the station. We hope those who stay will work with us since I don't think we'll survive if we don't."

There was nothing else to say. They could get some of them out on the 'vette if they packed them in tight, but it would be better to hire other ships. It wouldn't take too many creds to get people to the Freir system. The deckies could settle there if they wanted to, and if not, they could go wherever they wanted from the port.

The ensuing silence told her the decision wouldn't be made quickly. Some tossed suspicious glances her way. While Chill wanted them all to stand with her and the DEMC, they weren't members of her crew, so they had to make their own decisions.

Predictably, Shoviil was the first one to stand. He looked at the decky crews, who all nodded, then cleared his throat and addressed Chill. "I cannot speak for the mercenary crews who joined us over these past few weeks, but I do speak for the deckies. We aren't going anywhere. This is our home, and during the troubles we've faced together, you've shown us that we are supposed to fight for it. We'll find a way to keep it, whether the Jindahin like it or not."

The deckies murmured in agreement. Chill wondered if they understood the threat they would be facing if they stayed and were just being stubborn. However, they had stood their ground against the robot army of one of the most advanced AIs she'd ever seen. They'd known their cause was shaky, but they had fought on. That mindset was their culture at this point.

"We'll stick around," Shoviil continued. "We'll fight creepers. We'll fight bots. Fuck, send those Jindahin Janissaries against us, and we'll fight them too!"

That got an enthusiastic cheer from his people. Some of the mercs joined in.

Chill nodded and smiled. "We'll stand by you, however this ends."

"Happy to have the Dead Evil Mercenary Company on our side."

Surprisingly, that got a cheer too. The deckies could fight on their own, but they were looking at her like she was their leader.

She'd thought someone else would lead.

"We'll fucking fight," she called, nodding and raising a fist. "We'll clear this fucking station and keep it!"

The deckies and mercs roared. Some raised their weapons, while others held their fists up. To a being, they declared their intent to stand their ground, take the station, and keep it, no matter what came next.

Maybe she was getting better at this speech business. Practice was important. She still didn't know how they could stand against a fleet if the Jindahin tried to scrap the station, but Chill couldn't worry about that now. One step at a time.

Lugosh had thought the station would stand up to whatever the Jindahin threw at it. He had been rat-fuck crazy, but he might have had a point. She would look into that. If all went to plan and they found him with the creepers, she'd just ask him.

Chill doubted he would respond, though.

CHAPTER EIGHT

"How are we supposed to identify him?"

It was a good question, one Kortez had kept to himself for a while. They had to trap the right creeper. They didn't have the time or the resources to collect all the creepers and choose the ones who had the alpha strain.

Chill crossed her arms as she studied the footage the Janissaries had collected. The apparent commander of the creepers was larger than any of them, interestingly, and had greenery bulging from its body like any other creeper. It looked like a moss-covered statue, except it was moving and was carrying a weapon. The recording flicked to the rest of the creepers.

The footage demonstrated that the Janissaries had impressive reflexes. Their processing speed was much higher than hers—not a high bar since Chill thought she was just average. Their response times were considerably faster as well. It was interesting to watch, but the speed at which everything moved made her queasy.

"Their greenery is more extensive than the other creepers'," Chill commented. "Readings are different too. We're getting synaptic impulses from them. The rest of the creepers just have synaptic responses.

"It will be easy to spot them. The problem is getting near them. From what I can see, a small horde follows them everywhere. See where that one turns away? A whole flock of the fuckers turns with him. What do you think, Kharkanaw?"

Chill had wondered if she should talk to the Janissaries' commander without getting permission from the Over-Keeper, but they could apparently operate independently. When she'd contacted the commander to ask if he wanted to come look at the footage with her, he had responded enthusiastically.

It had been a day of surprises. The deckies deciding to stay to hold the station had been the first step. Standing their ground against the infestation would be the next.

The Janissaries would be critical for that.

Kortez replayed the recording from Kharkanaw's suit. "The way I see it, the problem isn't getting to the commander, although that's going to be tough. They know this station better than anyone, and they know how to get away quickly, so we have no advantage.

"The real problem is going to be reaching them without killing them. The rest of the creepers will act as a living shield, and if we shoot or blow our way in, we'll run the risk of catching our target in the crossfire."

Chill nodded. "That's why a trap is the best way. Corner the commander and its group of creepers in a spot where we have control of the variables and can get to it at our leisure."

"Why don't we just kill them all and get samples from the dead?" Kharkanaw asked, rewinding the footage so he could watch it again.

"We don't know how effective this alpha strain will be if the host is dead," Chill pointed out. "If we can't get one, we'll try the dead tissue to see if it works. No point in getting our hands on one of them, only to find out afterwards that we needed the fucker alive, though."

Kharkanaw nodded. On the recording, the creeper commander stepped in with a sword—really just a club with long, sharp metal pieces slotted into it—and slammed it into the head of one of the mercs who was fighting with the Janissaries. The rest of the creepers ran away.

"So, we'll try to take the fucker alive."

"We won't endanger our people to do it, though," Chill replied. "We'll need them all alive and well even if we are successful."

"To fight the approaching Jindahin fleet?"

She paused the vid and glanced at the Janissaries' commander. Chill was suddenly very aware that he was head and shoulders taller than her. Kortez could probably hold his own against the Dahin, but Kharkanaw would treat her like the Semper Clan leader and take her head off in one bite.

"You, ah, heard about that, did you?"

"I did."

"Going to do anything about it? Better to work out our issues now, right?"

Kharkanaw studied her for a few long seconds, then let

out a grunting laugh. "There will be no issues. I promise you that. I saw your speech to the deckies and the mercs. You did not hide it. I respect the position you are in and the decisions you have made. Standing against insurmountable forces when you know the odds is brave."

Chill blinked as she considered what he'd said.

"Just so there aren't any misconceptions in the future, are you saying you respect our efforts and look forward to giving us an honorable death in the name of the Jindahin Salifate?"

Her question got another chuckle from the Janissaries' commander. "Fuck, no. Janissaries join the order to serve a higher cause than the Salifate. We take orders, as most soldiers do, but when we find a righteous cause to fight for, it takes precedence over those. It is not a treasonous offense to fight for what is right, although I can assure you there are many among the Salifate high command who believe differently."

"So you meant—"

"We will fight alongside you against the infestation and against the Jindahin forces if such hostilities occur. We will stand by you to the end."

That was the second time he had referred to it in that manner. Good as it was to know the Janissaries—well, Kharkanaw—would fight with them, he apparently expected the fecal matter to hit the impellers.

"You don't think we're going to win," Chill pointed out, hitting play again.

Kharkanaw shrugged. "We enter every battle hoping to finally face the opponent who, by strength or wit, will defeat us. Isn't that the hope of every warrior? To fall amongst your slain foes, doing what you love?"

"Not sure about you, big fella," she countered. "I'd rather spend my last few days drinking something strong on a beach on a vacay planet while taut and tan beach boys oil my leathery hide."

Kharkanaw laughed again. This one was deeper, like he was mocking her. "You play a clever game. Maybe even with yourself, but I think I have your measure. War is in your veins, and battle rushes life through your gills. You've had plenty of opportunities to walk away from fights you likely will not win, yet you choose to stand your ground."

"I don't have gills." Chill avoided the point. "Besides, it is less loving the fight than having something worth fighting for that keeps me going. Not many people can stand up for themselves. Even if they can, they could use help. I simply provide a service and get paid well for it."

"You would have been paid a lot better by the people you were fighting against," Kharkanaw pointed out, rewinding the footage a few seconds to verify that what looked like another commander was just a creeper. "It is odd how you warriors keep finding good causes to fight for. It's almost like you go looking."

Chill raised a finger and opened her mouth to make a counterargument but realized she didn't have one. He had a point; they did keep picking the weird ones and sticking with the cause to the end, even if it wasn't the contracted end.

"I think I liked you better when you were just a faceless, towering mountain of Janissary." She shook her head and changed the subject. "You think we can get to one of those commanders?"

Kharkanaw returned his attention to the recording, then shook his head. "Doubt it. Creatures might be smart enough to know they can't be captured alive, so it'll kill itself before we can take it down. I don't think any of our stun measures will work on them. We'll end up with a dead commander. The Over-Keeper will have to deal with that."

"Now that we're on speaking terms," Chill said, changing the subject again, "how did you and your Janissaries get tied to him?"

"Long story," Kharkanaw answered. "We were operating on the front lines when we were ordered to operate as the front guard for an Over-Keeper and... Huh. I guess it's not that long a story."

"Orders? That's it?"

"Nothing else required. We've acted as bodyguards before. Sometimes it's because the higher-ups want to instill shock and awe. Other times, we have genuine threats to put down. In one case, a group of Janissaries was ordered to help a high-level member of the Salifate command steal objects of value from another official, who was keeping them well-guarded."

"Did they?"

"Yes, although it's unclear if they were offered a portion of the treasure in return for their breaking their oaths. They were prevented by a human warrior who used his smaller size to infiltrate the air vents in the building and picked them off one by one. As you can imagine, it was a massive embarrassment for the Janissary corps, so the story was quashed."

"Was selling their principles the embarrassment, or was it that an ordinary human took them down?"

"He was no ordinary human."

She supposed he had to say that. She doubted any human caught in the wrong place at the wrong time could take down an entire squad of Janissaries in full battle armor.

There had to be more to the story.

Before she could ask any more questions, however, Kharkanaw's beeper went off. He pressed the button, which resulted in a spate of what sounded like gibberish to her.

"The mutants are attacking again," he growled, seamlessly transforming from friendly giant to killing machine. The change was shocking. "A large attack, too. Feel free to join the defense effort."

She nodded. "Let's go. We'll get our suits and meet you and your men at the Vert's entrance."

"Make it so."

The Janissary left their loading bay and rushed over to where a pair of his men were waiting. Kortez and Ivan started climbing into their suits, and Chill did the same.

It was comforting to head into the thick of it in full mech armor with rifles instead of just their skins. Her cuts and scratches were healing, but they still itched.

She resolved to let someone else charge headfirst into the monsters next time.

The mutants had picked a point and were coming in numbers. The sounds of caster fire and explosions led them to where two Janissaries and a small group of mercs were holding the line.

They had set up behind a barricade, which gave them a meter and a half of high ground and cover to work with. Some mutants were trying to scale it, using the bodies of their fallen to form a ramp.

Others just climbed the backs of their comrades and tried to vault the barricade. A few got through, which forced a couple of the mercs to turn away from the defenses.

They'd gotten there just in time.

"Fucking shits," Kharkanaw growled. He threw a grenade into the mess of mutants on the other side of the barricade and directed a pair of his Janissaries to take out the mutants who got past.

Chill left them to secure the defenses and charged.

Kortez roared and rushed forward. Cortador carved through two mutants. Several sprouted knives in their legs, which slowed them down enough for Chill to approach, her hammer whining as it powered up. She took the head off the first as her rifle cleared out two more.

Another wave of mutants caught them before they could adjust, and Chill had to fend off three that grabbed and hacked at her arms and legs. They understood that they couldn't get through the thick armor around her chest and head.

It was painful, but they were immediately reinforced by Janissaries who formed a wall with their heavier armor and drove forward.

Chill swung her hammer and crushed a creeper's legs, then lowered her shoulder and ran over a second. The mech armor wasn't as heavy, versatile, or powerful as the

Janissaries' armor, but it was more than enough to run over something as small and squishy as a mutated body.

"Keep moving!" she shouted, then brought her hammer down on the head of a creeper and took a step back. Her rifle cut another group of the creatures off at the knees.

She just walked over the bodies as she advanced, especially when there were too many of them. It got dangerous when the downed mutants grabbed her as she pressed forward, but they didn't have the time to confirm kills.

When those without legs proved troublesome, she stomped them down. Like Ivan had said, they were much more satisfying to deal with than Scourge bots.

Or had that been Kortez? Maybe it had been her. It didn't matter. Chill advanced while protecting the flanks of the Janissary wall. Kortez and Ivan pushed forward and attacked. They had fought together for a long time, and Chill was jealous when she watched them work. They knew where the other would be without having to look and smoothly and instinctively protected each other's blind spots.

It would take a while for her to get to that point, but she was making progress. She'd recently charged down a narrow corridor without being impaled by any of Ivan's flying knives. That assumed none of her cuts and scratches had come from those knives. She hadn't watched the footage from the reclamation of their ship yet.

"Forward!" Kharkanaw's voice boomed through the chamber as the Janissary wall drove forward, crushing the horde they were fighting.

It was an odd time for the mutants to engage in such a committed attack. They'd already lost a hundred of their number, and it felt like the merc force hadn't made a dent. They still had plenty of ammo, however, and they kept pushing forward. Several of the Janissaries had set up heavy repeaters on the barricades, which decimated the mutants.

They had rockets too, although Chill assumed they had been warned not to use them in every fight. The Serpent had survived having one of its Verts compromised, but that didn't mean it would stand up to further punishment.

The self-repair systems on the station were working much slower now. Like the Scourge, they had relied on the networked nests to function.

"Chill!" Ivan kept his focus on the battle as he directed her attention to a point on the far side of the chamber. The area was overrun by creepers, but when she zoomed in on the point, something was off.

The creepers didn't show much respect for personal space, running each other over and clambering over any of their number that was too slow. The ones Ivan had highlighted were keeping their distance from one of the creepers—a large one with greenery sprouting from its body. They tried to avoid it, although the press of bodies made it inevitable that one would eventually step close to the creature, which was growling orders to the rest.

Without a second glance, the commander's sword hacked the creeper's head off.

Chill raised her rifle and aimed at the head of the commander. She doubted she could hit it from that distance, but she wanted to try. Making it obvious that she was trying to hit the commander, she paused for a few seconds before opening fire.

The mech suit gave her enough height to have a good shot, and she fired three rounds.

She smirked when all three rounds were intercepted by creepers throwing their bodies in the way. One would have been a coincidence. Even two. Five got in the way of the shots, two making sure the rounds didn't go through the first.

She had proven that the creepers would try to keep their commander alive. Whether out of fear, adoration, respect, or a combination of the three, they had put their bodies between bullets and a being that showed no compunction about cutting them down if they got too close.

That was an interesting point. Chill set her HUD to scan the creeper commander while she dealt with a surge of attacks directed at her. They pushed her back a step, which gave the Janissaries an opening.

While it was impossible to get a clear look at the commander, given all the greenery sprouting from its body, the body measurements matched the recordings of Lugosh. It was definitely a Dahin, and it was larger than any others of that race she'd met except the Janissaries. Either the infection had forced it to grow bigger, or the host had been a large specimen.

Chill doubted it was the former since it hadn't done the same thing to the other creepers. She could not get confirmation since there wasn't much of a face for her to scan. She doubted that getting closer would yield better results, either.

She hadn't believed Lugosh, whatever was left of him, had survived this long. He'd had to fight the Scourge, the deckies, and his own people, so the idea seemed absurd, but the evidence was stacking up.

Chill couldn't deny what she was seeing, but she didn't know Lugosh's whole crew, having only seen two. It was possible that he had had an enforcer who was his size. It could also be a Dahin who had arrived years later.

"Get ready!" Ivan called as he drew a handful of grenades out of his pouch.

She knew where that was going, but before she could remind him that they needed the commander alive, he tossed three into the closest group of creepers. The explosives went off with loud cracks that echoed through the chamber. The space filled with smoke and bits and pieces of the creepers that had been caught in the blast.

Then the scrubbers cleared the smoke, and she saw that many of the creatures had been struck by shrapnel. It was as good an opening as they would get. Chill lunged forward, gunning down nearby creatures to clear the way for the Janissaries. They churned through the creepers by gunning them down, hacking through them, or simply running over them.

They fought well together, working with those who had set up on the barricade like they had been operating together for decades.

She wondered how to drill for coordinated attacks. Maybe the only way to perfect it was years of practice. She was willing to accept that, but if there were shortcuts, she wanted to know.

The creepers didn't stick around. Ivan and his grenades had weakened them, and further attacks would be pointless. They slipped through vents and ports that should have been impossible to access and vanished into the labyrinthine station.

It was satisfying to kill them, and it was frustrating to watch them get away. It left her with a bitter taste in her mouth every time.

But they had more important matters to think about. Chill scanned the bodies, knowing she would find only creepers. Most were Dahin, although there was a smattering of other species. There was no sign of the commander.

She hadn't expected to find him. Her theory was the larger creeper had been the first to retreat. When it was safe, it ordered the rest to retreat.

On the one hand, it was good news that the commander was still alive despite Ivan's best attempts to kill him. On the other, it had gotten away. They'd missed their chance, and now they had to try to trap it. Killing it in this attack would have been too easy.

They had gotten good readings on it. They probably couldn't track its movements through the station, but they would know when it popped up to attack them again. Then they could set up a trap.

"All right." Chill watched as the station's systems started up cleaning the area. "Our work here is done."

"Your help was appreciated." Kharkanaw threw her a salute. "We can take it from here."

Chill gestured for her crew to join her.

"Do you really believe they'll join us in fighting the Jindahin fleet?" Kortez asked on their private channel.

"That's tomorrow's trouble," Chill told him. "We have to act as though we believe them."

"So, we don't *actually* believe them?" Ivan insisted.

"Fuck, no, but we're trying to be positive." She grinned. "If we want to make it out of here with friends on that side of the aisle, we should make a show of trusting them, right?"

The universe owed them some luck.

Not that she expected to get it.

CHAPTER NINE

"We don't have many options," Kortez commented, crossing his arms. "We're starting to learn how they choose their targets."

Chill nodded. "From what I could tell, it attacked that point to reach the antechamber, and it only attacked the moment those mercs relieved the Janissaries who were holding that position. They were only slowed down because the Janissaries heard the sounds of fighting coming from their defensive position. If they had attacked a few minutes later, that chamber probably would have been lost, and we would have been fighting with our backs to the secured antechamber. We'd have all those turrets to help us, but we would have had nowhere to retreat if the fighting didn't go our way."

"You don't think the Over-Keeper would have opened the doors to let us in?" Ivan asked.

"Hell, I wouldn't put it past him to turn his turrets on us if it meant clearing the room," Kortez grumbled. "We have to get the monsters to attack. We won't get one of those fuckers to show up at a well-defended position, and we can't wait for them to find a weak point in our defenses. We might not have the Janissaries that close to help us the next time it happens."

Chill nodded. "We'll have to poke a hole in our defenses to draw them in."

"Just find a hole the creepers would exploit and set our trap there," Ivan suggested. "It could be the Janissaries already know of the weaknesses in the fortress that they helped to set up and therefore would be willing to help us."

Chill shook her head. "For one thing, they likely picked up on those weak points and alerted the Over-Keeper about them, and he's already working on clearing them up. If a weak point now, it'll be something they hadn't accounted for, like the weaknesses in their outer defenses. Even then, the creepers will avoid points the Janissaries are patrolling."

Kortez scowled. "So, what's your idea? You want us to break our defenses and hope we can draw them in? We'll need to make it convincing enough that they don't suspect a trap and send Lugosh. It will also have to be functional so we can spring the trap when he is inside."

"We don't want to lose any vital points on the station while we're retreating," Ivan chimed in. "I mean, it's supposed to look good, but not too good. If it's smart enough to probe our defenses, it'll know when we're playing dead."

Kortez and Chill nodded. "Fuck," she muttered. "This isn't the kind of situation I wanted to be in."

Ivan shrugged. "We could wait for another opportunity for an attack. If it doesn't happen soon enough, we'll just have to explain to the Jindahin that if they want to take their fucking station back, they can do it on their own time."

Chill scratched her chin as she called up the virtual map of the whole station, scowling as she inspected their options. "It's going to have to be more layered than that. They won't attack if they think we're drawing them in. They're too smart, as we've already established."

"Layered?" Kortez raised an eyebrow quizzically. "You want to give them multiple points to attack?"

"No." She called up a handful of points. "That's where the most mutant activity has registered on our sensors. They are also the points where the life support systems have been functional longest, which indicates those are the areas where the mutants have set their little civilized corners of the Serpent. Attacking from all points might be enough to reduce its intellect."

"Hold up. You want to attack the areas of the station where the mutants are the most numerous?" Kortez shook his head. "We're supposed to be drawing them into a trap, not getting everyone killed."

"A coordinated effort might distract the fuckers," Ivan countered. "It's not the safest way for us to do this, but safe ways will take a lot longer than two weeks. Besides, if we commit forces to the attack, it might make the fuckers think we're leaving other areas undefended. That would make it easier to draw them in."

"Are we really considering this?" Kortez highlighted the treasure vault/fortress. "If all goes well, we will catch the fuckers with their trousers around their ankles. If it doesn't, we'll be committing a massive part of our forces to a fight we don't expect to win."

"It would have to be on a volunteer basis," Chill answered. She zoomed in the projection by waving her hand. "We'll have to see about correcting this shit. Maybe buy some new equipment."

"Sorry about that." Alex spoke through the speakers. "The equipment is outdated."

"No worries. I wasn't blaming you." Chill cleared her throat. "We need to update the hardware on the ship. Anyway, where was I? Oh, right. We're going to need volunteers for the attack missions, and we'll have to bolster the Janissaries with merc crews. I'm thinking we'll use the ones who won't be tempted by being so close to the treasure room that they'll try to make some extra creds."

"The established crews," Kortez agreed. "None of the eager young bucks looking to make their careers with big and flashy moves. The ones who have a reputation for being contract-focused. Determined to get the work done, no more and no less than what their contract demands."

"There aren't a lot of those around," Chill muttered. "The established crews didn't pack their shit and wander out here. Still, there have to be a couple around."

"You know who could help us with that?" Kortez grinned. "I'm happy to have Shoviil take charge. Better that we're not dealing with all the different parties like we did on Mugh-9."

"Shoviil has been doing an excellent job of organizing the decky and mercenary crews and keeping them all as busy as they want to be. Of course, I've been helping him keep track of the crews who want to be on duty. I'm also picking up on complaints and compliments, and setting up the crews who like working together on the same shifts, and the compensation, although the Over-Keeper prefers to handle that. I understand why, but it's not an efficient use of his resources. I am more than capable of ensuring all teams are properly compensated for the time they've worked."

Chill nodded. "All right, so you know which crews have the parameters we'll need. Are there any?"

"One moment."

Kortez crossed his arms as the AI started compiling the data. "How do you think she's going to factor in all the variables?"

"I'll help with that," Dorian announced on the intercom. "It's difficult to add everything, but I think we've got a handle on it."

Ivan smirked. "You think he's ever going to leave the cockpit?"

"Why would I?" Dorian countered, having heard the question. "The chairs are a lot more comfortable now that I got new ones, and it's the most secure location on the ship."

"You know you can lock your cabin from the inside too, right?" Chill asked.

"Which is why I'm keeping all my shit there. Between visits to my cabin, the kitchen, and the cockpit, I should be safe until we get off this fucking station."

Chill nodded. She wanted to tell him to grow up, but she sometimes wished she could hole up and let the rest of the galaxy pass her by too. Unlike her, Dorian could do that while doing the job he had been hired to do. He had already gone above and beyond what was expected of him, considering his developing piloting skills.

"Right," Kortez mumbled. "We're not going to have a lot of people to choose from. We're also going to have to ask if the Janissaries are willing to work with the merc companies we pick for them. I have a feeling they'll disapprove of some of our choices."

They could only hope the small pool of candidates Alex had earmarked would perform as they were supposed to. Greed could make those who otherwise would have just otherwise just done the job ambitious. Sentient behavior was difficult to predict.

Chill wasn't an anthropologist, but many papers had been written about the various sentient species' responses to stimuli. She had read that it was because many shared a common ancestor, although nobody agreed on what that ancestor had been. It was a controversial topic and one she was not interested in debating. Those discussions ended in violence.

"All right," Chill growled, rolling her shoulders. "Looks like we have our candidates. Nothing's going to get done if we just sit around and wait for shit to happen."

"I assumed you would make a move, so I've messaged Commander Kharkanaw and Shoviil," Alex informed her.

"This should be an interesting conversation." Chill grimaced. "You think we can meet with them in person to discuss the plan?"

"The commander has sent word to say he very much wants to join you in the discussions," Alex answered. "Shoviil has yet to reply, but from his schedule, he might not have his communicator on him."

"Then we should do him the courtesy of taking this little party to him." Chill nodded for Ivan and Kortez to follow her as she left the ship and walked to where Shoviil had set himself up with a small command center of his own.

She still didn't know what crew the Xo had been part of. Chill remembered fighting them and the Janissaries stepping in to kill them all when they were trying to surrender, yet nobody ever talked about it.

Although the deckies were divided into crews like the mercs, there was no loyalty. People from one crew could jump to another crew without eliciting much of a response. If a crew leader was killed, the rest picked another crew or started their own. She didn't know how they picked the leaders but pick they did.

Her thoughts made her wonder why they all followed Shoviil's orders. Probably because he had the most access to the DEMC and the Over-Keeper, so everyone listened to him. If one of the others got involved, they might listen to that person instead.

It was a fluid society, and the rules were not clear-cut. It seemed as though they didn't understand it themselves and just went with the flow.

Shoviil, however, deserved his position. He took a percentage of the earnings, but he wasn't greedy, although he had made a small fortune from facilitating the others' work. He fought too, but he was not on any of the crews.

Chill would ask him about it when they had time. Hopefully, while she was flying to a new opportunity after they'd cleared the station and the Jindahin had worked a deal out with the deckies to allow them to stay since they knew the Serpent better than anyone else. She was not hopeful about the second part, though.

Shoviil spotted them approaching and opened the door of the building his office was in. It was the one the Sempers had claimed, although he hadn't taken over the entire space. Other crews also used it as their headquarters. He'd set himself up next to one of the larger server rooms so he could share his databases with Alex.

He didn't split his server with the other crews. It was unclear whether he'd used his superiority to keep them away or if they didn't know about it. She didn't ask.

He directed them into his workspace. "Nice to see you again. I've looked at your plan. Well, it's not much of a plan yet. You really think a flurry of attacks will distract our enemies to the point where we can draw them into a trap?"

"I thought it was a better option than waiting for the creepers to attack and hoping we could steer the fight into an area where we could trap a commander. If we force them into action, we'll have more control over what happens, as well as luring them into areas they might think we're leaving undefended. If you have a better idea, I would be glad to hear it."

Shoviil grinned. "That's what I like about the three of you. You're willing to let someone else take the lead. I don't have a better plan in mind. Still, we'll be committing a lot of our troops to an attack we don't have much control over."

Chill nodded. "That's why I needed your input, as well as Kharkanaw's."

"Alex told me he was on his way over. Does he know you plan to join us in our fight against the Jindahin if they consider the deckies as a threat that needs to be cleared out?"

"Yes." She narrowed her eyes. "He watched my information session, and he says he and the Janissaries will fight on our side if that happens."

"Really?"

She shrugged. "That's what he said."

"You believe him?"

"Not necessarily, but at the moment, we can't afford to make enemies out of our allies. We'll be watching them for a double-cross, though."

"Wise, although he's probably anticipating that."

"Obviously."

It was odd to be discussing the commander while watching him approach on the cameras and sensors in Coil Cove. Kharkanaw and the Janissaries had set up a base around the remains of their ship. They weren't allowed to deploy around the Over-Keeper's fortress.

"Can I ask you something?" Chill kept her eyes on the screen. The general question had been on her mind since before they'd met Shoviil.

"Sure."

"Don't answer if it's too personal."

Shoviil grinned. "What's the question?"

"Why did you remove your feather crest?"

His grin disappeared. It was clear the Xo hadn't been expecting *that* question. He ran his fingers over the jagged scars where his crest had been. "What brought that on?"

"Feel free to ignore it. I just...I could never consider removing one of my sensory organs. Humans have removed eyes or tongues or ears for ritual purposes during our history, but I would never do it."

"It wasn't a choice." He shrugged. "I was a criminal looking at a wipe, and I managed to break out with some help from my family. They were all Xo, so I wouldn't be accepted among them if I wasn't. My circumstances are quite common among those who make the decision—family pressure and being ostracized by the rest of our people. Some choose to do it as a direct insult to the Authority, but they are far less common these days."

"Okay." Chill sighed. It was another example of the kinds of social implications rigid social structures carried. It was a powerful evolutionary strength, but it wasn't without its drawbacks.

Especially if the civilization was led by idiots, which Chill believed was true of most of the leaders of humanity.

"What about that scar on your cheek?"

Chill blinked at the sitting Xo. "It's…"

"Come on. I answered your personal question. Fair's fair. You have to answer mine."

He was right. Fair *was* fair. She hadn't thought the situation through.

"I got in a fight with someone considerably larger than I was," she answered. "They cracked me across the cheekbone hard enough to break the bone and rip the skin. I ended up getting a steel plate underneath. Instead of stretching the skin to cover the spot, I elected to have it grafted onto the bone replacement. It's a reminder that what fails to kill me makes me stronger."

Besides, the graft had been cheaper than the surgery. It also represented one of the first times she'd ever gotten back at someone who beat her. She'd picked her moment, and the asshole had ended up in an XTA prison. She had made sure he would get wiped and spend the rest of his life mining resin. She'd stopped keeping track of him after the third year, but she did check in occasionally to make sure he was still there.

It was another reminder of how vindictive she could be when pushed. That side of her came out to play when she needed it, but it had been a while.

Thankfully, the questions stopped when Kharkanaw reached them. He didn't slow down for the doors, just went through them while they were opening. Shoviil had to open the last door early to keep the Janissary from walking into it.

"The AI told me to meet you here," he growled.

"Got a problem with those, do you?" Shoviil countered.

"They are useful tools." The Dahin changed the subject. "We are going to attack the mutants. I approve. How are we going to do it?"

He *was* a warrior.

"We'll attack them to keep them from focusing on what we are doing to draw them in. That way, if they find a weak point in our defenses, they'll jump on it to press their advantage."

Kharkanaw shrugged. "I follow that logic. Sort of. We'll need to change our strategies to make things more interesting from our end."

"We were playing it slow and methodical by claiming as much territory as we could hold onto and waiting for more mercs to arrive." Chill sighed. "Things have changed. We need results more than ever."

"Do you think we can predict what will happen next with those things?" Shoviil countered, looking at the rest of the people in the room. "For all we know, the monsters are just waiting for us to make this kind of move so they can crush us."

"We have to risk it." Kortez shrugged. "Being aggressive is all we have left. Otherwise, we'll be stuck clearing this station for decades. While I'm happy to have steady work, I don't think the Jindahin are going to fund us that long."

"I like it," the Janissary replied. "It's about time my men and I went in to stomp the fucking mutants into paste."

"A few of them might, but we'll need most of you in reserve for when we spring the trap to catch Lugosh or whatever other monster we're dealing with."

Kharkanaw scowled. "You really think Lugosh is the mutants' commander?"

"Might well be." Chill rubbed her temples. "At this point, I will believe anything I have to to get the fucking job done."

"All right." Ivan crossed his arms. "Now, Commander, do you have any thoughts about how you want this to play out? Any specific mercs you want or don't want at your side?"

Kharkanaw nodded as he tapped at the screen to make it larger so the rest of them could see it. He hadn't asked Shoviil if he could touch the equipment.

"Wait!" Chill interrupted, leaning closer. "When did Dorian give you control of the slaved mechs?"

Shoviil smiled. "You know I run a tight ship, but we're going to need extra muscle closer to Coil Cove. The kid thinks you won't be using the mechs much, so he passed them to me. I assumed you had signed off on it."

"I thought Dorian was using them to keep the ship safe," Ivan muttered. "After the mutants' attack, he's been... protective of the ship and his place in it. He doesn't want to risk losing it to another attack. Wait, *you're* running a tight ship?"

Shoviil grinned. "I've been keeping the mercs and deckies busy. Let me show you."

"I think we should keep our attention on the matter at hand," Kharkanaw interrupted before Shoviil could show them all the work he'd been doing.

"Well, let us know if there's anything you need us for," Chill commented, suddenly realizing they had been left out of all the planning. Kortez and Ivan nodded, realizing the same thing.

"That's fine," Shoviil assured them. "You've been showing us how to do this for a while now. Time for us to show you we're all quick learners."

Chill narrowed her eyes. "We don't fit in on that tight ship you're running, right?"

"Well, there is that, but it doesn't mean the other is less true."

CHAPTER TEN

Chill was starting to have some doubts. Sometimes things worked out the way they were supposed, but it didn't mean it would this time. Especially given the number of variables they couldn't account for.

"You're doing it again."

"Doing what?" Chill asked and looked up from her screen.

"We've learned to recognize that when you're staring at something but not doing anything with that furrowed brow, you're thinking about something bad," Dorian answered with a small smile. "It's going to work out, and even if it doesn't, we'll make it work anyway. That's our thing. We try shit. It goes wrong. We adapt and keep on fighting and end up on top. Or alive, I guess. That works out to 'on top' in my book."

She smiled at him, then leaned back in her seat and scanned the readings from the station. "I'm glad you have so much faith. *I'm* wondering if we haven't played our last gambit. Even if we survive this, Lugosh might slip away again. Then we've let them know we're capable of pulling this kind of trick. It won't work again."

"Then we'll come up with another one." Dorian tapped her shoulder with his fist. "Zichix told me you've been under a lot of stress lately. Time to let go. What happens will happen. Worrying about how bad shit can get will only weaken your heart."

"Weaken my heart?"

"Yes. It's well-established that stress is a contributing factor in congestive heart failure. I forget the exact terminology, but stressing about shit you can't change is how you end up clutching your chest and dying on the shitter."

"That's a very specific example. Does a member of your family have a history of heart disease, and that's why you know so damn much about it?"

Dorian grinned. "Please, my family is *the* history of heart disease. On my rich fucker of a father's side, of course. My half-Suid mother is still alive."

"Your father got it on with a half-Suid?" Chill tilted her head. "He's more open-minded than I am, although it's mostly the tusks. I'd be worrying about how they could cut into me."

"I think it's less about open-mindedness and more about a fetish. It doesn't matter. The point is, Suids are amazingly resistant to stress. That's what she told me, anyway."

Talking was distracting her, which was good. They were just sitting around, waiting for everything else to go right in case their trap had to be sprung. Their ship would *be* the trap if everything went to hell. That didn't fill her with the confidence she needed for the fight, and she couldn't help but think about the many ways this could go badly.

Talking about Suids and their history of heart disease —or the lack thereof—got her mind off the rest. Chill rubbed her temples as her team monitored the fighting elsewhere on the station.

"Sounds like it's going pretty well," Chill whispered, scanning the sensors and cameras that were keeping them updated.

Three incursion squads, each led by a pair of Janissaries, were heading toward the center of the mutants' civilization. They had orders that if the resistance was too stiff, they were to back off.

On the one hand, if the station's troops kept pushing, the mutants would fight back. If the troops retreated, the creatures' predator instincts would be triggered, and they would chase the fighters.

The station troops' job was to make themselves nuisances. They were advancing and taking down serious numbers of mutants with negligible casualties. "Negligible" sounded heartless, but this attack involved upward of three hundred people. Three dead and four injured was an acceptable number of losses.

She hoped she didn't get used to thinking that way since she was dealing with living beings. Thinking of them only as numbers would let her throw their lives away casually.

Two dozen fighters, Janissaries and a few mercs, stood their ground, waiting for the signal. Chill wondered how people felt in Coil Cove station since they were close enough to hear the shooting or at least the explosions. The ground shook and grav functions were going haywire across the station, contributing to the unsettling nature of their attack.

"Looks like we have their attention," Chill commed to the fighters. "Commander, that is your opening."

"Working on it."

The signals from the fortress were going haywire as well. An accidental explosion was difficult to pull off, especially in the tight confines of a station, but they would make it work. Ivan had teamed up with one of the Janissaries who knew explosives, and they'd set it up to look like a containment issue.

Just like that, the defenses set up around the fortress went down, and smoke filled the area.

"I love my job," Ivan whispered, watching the explosives going off. "I made it look like those plasma cannons our Over-Keeper friend is using as turrets overheated the electrical system, which runs too close to the gas feeds. It's the kind of thing that would have happened anyway if he kept those turrets running for another...say, three months. I doubt even the Janissaries would have seen it coming. It pays to have engineering knowledge."

"Why do I get the feeling you've pulled something like this before?" Dorian asked.

"Because he has," Chill answered. She glanced at Kortez, who was nodding. "Nothing on this scale, but there's a lot of smoke, fire, and attention. It was a sloppy blow, which will get Lugosh's notice."

Ivan tapped at his nose. "I appreciate you learning the lingo, but a blow means…well, it has a lot of other meanings. I would personally call it a dirty blow."

"Why is that better?" Ivan asked.

"It's not... You know what? Never mind. What are we looking at when we go in?"

Chill called up the requested data. "The dock gives us a clean approach. Between Dorian and Alex, I think we can get the commander in there. It'll be on us to keep the mutants from escaping, but we can't approach before we have confirmation that Lugosh or one of the commanders is onsite."

"Are there more commanders?" Dorian asked.

"Footage only gives us one of the fuckers at a time," Chill muttered, watching the Janissaries and mercs scrambling to set their defenses back up after the explosion. "It's hard to tell if there is more than just the one, but I feel like however many they have will oversee the defenses if Lugosh shows up to give us the business."

Kortez nodded. "You think Lugosh will show up because he wants to get his treasure back."

"That's my theory. He's tried to get into his vault over the decades. He might not even know why. That was why the area around the vault was overgrown when we got there. It doesn't matter what my theory is, though, especially if it's wrong."

Kortez chuckled. "We're starting to believe you when you get those theories. They aren't always right, but you've always got a bead on *something* even when you are wrong about the specifics."

She scowled as she keyed the comm. "Commander, you're supposed to make it look like you're getting everything back in order, but you're not *really* supposed to get everything back in order. If there are turrets up and running, they'll see through our little trap, and all this will have been for nothing."

"Copy that."

It was a gamble. They'd mapped every approach to the area so they knew where the attacks would be coming from and how they would be directed. They were supposed to make it look easy but not stupid-simple. They were also supposed to give enough ground to draw the commander into the trap without being overrun.

The Janissaries would have their hands full with most of the turrets being down. Chill insisted they keep a few functional so they had some firepower to fall back on, even though the Janissaries had insisted they could handle it.

She trusted their skills, but they didn't know how these creatures attacked. Nothing could be left to chance. If it didn't go their way, Chill wanted to make sure they kept the vault.

Hedging their bets seemed silly, but their employer was inside that vault and refused to leave it. They'd rubbed each other the wrong way, but he *was* their employer. She wouldn't risk his safety, even if he was willing to be put at risk.

"We have contact," one of the Janissaries announced over the comm. "Get ready for a fight, boys. Looks like a big mutant."

Life signs were surging toward the unprotected area around the vault like they had been waiting for something like this to happen before pressing in.

She scowled as fighting erupted around the vault. It was a chaotic mess from all angles, so it was difficult to tell what was happening. There was smoke and body parts, but most of their sensors had gone down, which made it difficult to determine what they were looking at.

"Shit," Chill whispered as she flipped through the feeds. "I can't see anything. Kharkanaw, you'll have to make the call for when we approach."

"I will."

He was surprisingly calm, given the fighting going on around him. The mutants were proving to be inventive. Some had strapped armor to their bodies, which kept them from being taken out immediately as they entered the line of fire. That allowed those coming up from behind to use the ones in front as shields as they advanced.

There had been no stipulations against explosives since there was no need to keep the station intact if they were going to lose it anyway. They had to assume the station could take the heat they were dishing out.

"All right, time to pull back," she whispered, watching the Janissaries work smoothly with their mercenary counterparts. Mercs were unpredictable, but the teams had been picked based on who would work together the best.

The troops retreated, leaving behind mines to slow the monsters down and keep them off their backs.

"We have Lugosh in sight!" Kharkanaw announced. "He's leading the pack forward!"

It was as clear an indicator as they would get. Chill motioned for Dorian to act as they headed to the loading bay. Ibu had their suits prepped and ready to go.

"Heading in now," Dorian announced as the ship moved. The shift in inertia always confused her since the dampers were supposed to take care of it.

Chill climbed smoothly into her suit, the armor

comforting as it encased her. It was like a second skin, but not quite. It was closer now, though. She was quickly adapting to using the suit.

"How long until we close the gap?" She asked after she'd run the checks on her suit.

"T-minus five minutes," Dorian announced. The station's grav acted on the ship, shifting their perception of "down" for a few seconds.

They heard the shooting from outside, and slugs pinged across their armor. Since the mutants weren't firing, the Janissaries and the mercs clearly didn't understand that the ship would help them by sealing the gap and limiting the places the monsters could retreat through.

There were still avenues, however. The active turrets would slow them down, but they had to act fast. They were trying to take out the monsters without killing the commander. Without killing Lugosh.

He *was* one of them, though. He could take a lot of damage without dropping, although Chill wouldn't risk causing his death until their boots were on the deck.

Dorian backed the ship into the thick of the fighting and closed off the main exit. It would be on Dorian and Alex to keep the ship steady and in place until the fighting stopped. For the moment, all they had to do was get clear.

Thankfully, whoever had been shooting at them stopped. Chill pressed the attack and Kortez and Ivan held up the flank, throwing themselves forward. That let Dorian close the bay doors behind them.

"Looks like we have a fight on our hands, boss!" Kortez shouted, sounding very happy about what he was doing.

Chill had considered giving him Blitz's hammer when

the dust settled. Charging into battle with Cortador and a hammer was a recipe for him to either become one of the most feared melee fighters in the galaxy or die very quickly and very badly.

She knew Kortez, but she didn't know which it would be. She'd therefore elected to make the decision after they were off the station. She slashed a pair of creatures out of the way, clearing a space for the hammer to crush the creepers behind them.

A skull shattered with a soft crunch, and a path opened through the mutants. They were still focused on the station troops, unaware that the trap had snapped shut.

"How's it going in there, Dorian?" Chill asked. Kortez rushed in ahead of her, cutting and carving his way through the monsters in front. That enabled Ivan to take those behind out with his knives, which made for easy pickings as she cruised forward.

"It would be a lot better if I could use our guns," Dorian muttered.

"The plasma rounds might melt the walls, which would give Lugosh an escape route. We're here to capture him, not melt him. No turrets. Just keep the fucking ship in place. Nothing will get through the armor, and as long as you keep it in place, nothing will get past you."

Chill didn't know if the creepers could escape by tearing through the walls, but the station leaders were assuming they couldn't. They hadn't seen them try that tack.

She advanced on the position Lugosh was holding. Most of the monsters were standing their ground there, but they had just keyed in on the attack from behind, so more creatures rushed in to try to stop them. Kortez just ran them over, letting his suit do the work. His knife and rifle finished them off while Chill and Ivan cleared the way for him.

It wasn't easy, but the fighting was going their way, and she had eyes on Lugosh for the first time since they started their little endeavor.

"He's rabbiting!" Chill shouted. The powerful-looking figure spotted them and turned around. It saw through their trap much faster than the rest of the creepers had. It gave them one look before sprinting away.

"He's what?" Ivan asked.

"Rabb…he's running! Running! Kharkanaw, clear us a path. We're going after him!"

"Working on it!"

The portable turrets came online and opened fire on the horde of creepers, cutting them down by the legs. It wasn't as clear a path as they could have hoped for, but the corridors were jam-packed with mutants, so the help was deeply appreciated. Ivan rolled a couple of grenades across the deck ahead of them, and bits and pieces hit the walls.

Chill jumped through the smoke, not caring that shrapnel stuck out of her armor. She headed after the fleeing commander.

"Why are we rushing in?" Kortez asked, sounding out of breath. "I mean, we have the whole place shut down, right?"

"We think so, but the asshole apparently doesn't feel the same way."

"Oh. Right."

The commander was heading for the sewers. They should have considered it would since they had ended up in them during their first fight on the station. They could use them too, assuming they were clear now that the Scourge wasn't maintaining the tunnels.

A group of mutants followed it down. It was interesting that Lugosh would retreat and pull its better troops away from the battle. It apparently didn't mind leaving the rest to be torn to pieces by the Janissaries, who were now pushing forward with the help of their turrets.

It was the job of Chill and her crew to catch it now, so the others no longer needed to pretend they were retreating. More of the turrets came online, melting through the creepers' front lines. That left her, Ivan, and Kortez with nothing to do but catch up with those who were leaving the party early.

"Ivan!" Chill called.

"Yeah, yeah. I'm on it."

They could have used Dorian and his trick shooting in the narrow confines of the sewers, but Ivan was throwing knives along the straight path they were pushing creepers down.

A couple of the commander's honor guard got in the way, but one of the knives slipped past and sank deep into the back of the former Dahin's thigh.

The mutations didn't help, although the greenery coming out of its skin might heal it quickly.

They had stopped it for the moment, or rather, slowed it since it was limping on its functional leg while the second dragged behind. Another pair of daggers flew toward its other leg. One went high and glanced off the side of its thigh, but the other cut through its Achilles tendon, or what passed for that construct in a Dahin. It didn't stop Lugosh, but it did trip it. It slammed into the deck and rolled a few times before coming to a halt.

A deep, low groan echoed through the tunnel. It sounded angry, and there was an immediate response from the other creepers in the tunnel. They halted and turned around, then rushed at her team with renewed vigor and rage, screeching and howling alien words that needed no translation. Rushing headfirst into armored mechs was all the translation she needed.

Kortez got through them, hacking at their corpses as the commander got to its feet. It was clear that it couldn't run. Standing and fighting were its only options. While Chill didn't think even a larger Dahin could stand against three mechs, its glowing green eyes sent a chill down her spine.

Kortez didn't pause. He just pushed forward and launched his suit at Lugosh.

It moved out of the way with a deft sidestep, which it should not have been able to do with one of its legs hamstrung. Kortez recovered and his armored fist crashed into the creature's side, sending it staggering into the wall of the tunnel.

Lugosh seemed unfazed by the strike, though it grabbed Kortez's hand and stopped him from bringing Cortador down. It followed that impressive feat by pushing on Kortez's faceplate with the other hand, growling and groaning as it forced the mech back.

"Some fucking help?" Kortez hissed, straining against the power of the creature they were trying to subdue, not kill.

"Right!" Chill had her knife out as well. She jumped in

and brought the blade down on the hand on Kortez's faceplate.

There was a surprising amount of resistance from the skin, but the suit's augmentation drove it through and cut the arm off just below the shoulder.

The mutant seemed surprised by her attack. It looked at its arm like it couldn't understand how the limb had been removed.

Kortez still couldn't get his hand free, but Ivan leaped in and took that arm off as well.

The creature had literally been disarmed.

Thick greenery covered the mutant's skin, though sections of armor had been bolted to its flesh to protect it.

"Appreciate it," Kortez muttered, finally prying off the hand that was still gripping his after it had been cut off. "Would have appreciated it sooner, mind, but still."

"We thought you had it," Ivan countered, ducking a wild attack by the still very much alive Lugosh, who was swinging his stumps at him. "But since you asked so pathetically for help, how could we leave you on your own?"

"Very fucking funny." Kortez's tone indicated he thought it was anything but.

They still had to decide what they were going to do.

"His wounds are already closed," Chill commented, watching Lugosh swinging at him. "If we connect the arms, they'll probably fuse back into his flesh."

"We might have had a harder time if we were dealing with the actual Lugosh," Kortez added, carefully cutting the other hamstring. "The virus ate his mind."

Chill scowled. The creature was still attacking, and it

had impressive strength and speed. They'd had a hard time catching up to it even in their suits, and its sheer power made it difficult to know what they were looking at.

It didn't matter. To accomplish their goals, they had to bring back what remained of this Dahin, Lugosh or not, to be tested.

"Right," Chill hissed, then grabbed the thick greenery and lifted the creature off the deck, even though it writhed to free itself. "Grab the asshole's arms. We don't want to leave bits of it behind so they can…fuck, I don't know—grow another Lugosh or something."

Kortez winced. "Yeah, probably a good idea. Ivan, you take one, I take the other?"

"Why do I—"

"Fuck it. Both of you, just grab the fucking arms!" Chill scowled at the creature, which was fighting to escape her grasp with a lot more vigor than she would have expected from something missing both arms and was hamstrung.

They had expected something to be weird about this situation, and this qualified.

"He's not as cold and calculating as the Dahin we saw in the vids," Chill muttered, relenting and grabbing one of the legs as it fought to free itself. "You'd think there would be a lot more to the commander leading all the fucking monsters on this station to kill us, right?"

Ivan shrugged. "That infection had an effect on his mind. It might have destroyed the non-essential bits, leaving just enough of the old Lugosh to keep spreading the infection."

"I don't care." She shook her head. "We need to get it back to the Treasure Keeper and see if it can find a cure."

CHAPTER ELEVEN

"Are you sure that's right?" Chill asked as she shifted the mutant into the cell. She shouldn't have been surprised that the vault had one, but she hadn't expected it until the Over-Keeper directed her to take what remained of Lugosh to it and sealed the door behind it.

The door was fortified glass that revealed what was happening inside. Added circuits tracked the inmate in case it could camouflage itself.

"How did the capture go?" Kuzratha asked after Lugosh was secured.

"He was uncooperative," Chill answered. The mutant had stopped fighting. It didn't even make a try for the door, simply watching them through the glass. "Almost ripped Kortez out of his armor."

"That's not what happened," Kortez countered.

"It had your hand pinned and was pushing you back by the faceplate," Ivan reminded him. "How would you describe that?"

"Fuck off. How's that?"

"Well-put." Ivan grinned.

"Can we get back on topic?" Chill asked.

Kuzratha nodded. "Indeed. It would be interesting to know how the mutations allowed a biological creature to stand against a hydraulic-powered mech suit."

"Yeah, we wondered that too," Chill muttered. "We're going to look into the possibility of the hydraulics systems having been compromised in the fighting beforehand. Another possibility is that the mutation creates a biological system stronger than one powered by hydraulics, although considerably less durable."

Kuzratha nodded. "Indeed. I noticed you removed his arms. Was that so we could acquire samples of him without having to enter the chamber?"

"Yes." She raised an eyebrow at Kortez. "Wasn't to save Kortez from having his head ripped off or anything like that."

"Fuck. Off."

"What were you saying before?" Ivan asked, staring at the creature inside the cell. "Who is sure what is right?"

"Dorian was telling me that the incursions into the mutants' territory are going well," Chill answered. "There are other ways for us to retake the station, but I doubt all-out aggression is the solution. We have more people now, but the infestation is one of the most overwhelming enemies we've ever faced."

Kortez pulled his helmet off and scowled. "I don't know. The mutants probably didn't expect us to attack them in force. That, or they were hoping to catch us with our pants down and over-extended themselves, and now they're scrambling."

Chill could not disregard that possibility, yet she couldn't shake the feeling that something was up. She took a deep breath and focused on their next actions. Nothing would make her happier than introducing the cure into the air scrubbers, but it was all playing out too well.

"Dorian, are you watching what's happening on the front lines?" Chill asked over the comm. "What are they looking at in terms of resistance?"

"Let me check." He paused, likely distracted by a game.

She couldn't blame him for keeping himself occupied during the incursion. The game was probably more interesting since he couldn't fight himself. If he was playing that erotic game again, she would block the suggested vids that came up on the ship's shared account.

"They're pushing forward hard," Dorian answered. "Nothing's going to stop them, from what I'm seeing. The mutants have the numbers, but they started retreating almost immediately."

"*Almost* immediately?" Chill looked around. "Seems like they're not really trying to defend. Slow us down, maybe."

Kortez grinned. "The monsters are being blown to pieces without their leader."

"That's not how it works," Ivan muttered. "I don't think so, anyway. I mean, we *are* carrying explosive backups to make sure the creatures can't hold a position without taking heavy losses, but the monsters do have survival instincts. Not the kind that we do, but still. Since there's no leader, maybe they just don't want to charge into the Janissaries' charnel house."

There was no need to overthink it. If the fighting was going well, they shouldn't complain.

Still, the Lugosh mutant wasn't reacting the way she thought it would be to being imprisoned. It had fought tooth and nail to escape her grasp, but now that it was in a cell, it was standing calmly at the very center, staring at them through the glass door.

Calm staring was always the worst kind. It locked eyes with anyone who met its gaze to make its stay as uncomfortable for them as it could. Not as uncomfortable as what they had put it through, but it could have killed Kortez if she hadn't dismembered it.

"How long should we wait to get word that we don't need to bother with a cure because the whole infestation is gone?" Kortez asked, leaning against the wall. He was perfectly comfortable staring Lugosh down.

Chill scowled as the AI started the necessary scans of their prisoner, though calling it a prisoner wasn't accurate. There were rules about how prisoners of war were to be treated, and chopping the arms off prisoners to contain them was against those rules.

"So, what are we doing?" Chill asked.

"Are you talking to me?" Dorian asked.

"Nope. Talking to the AI."

"Me?" Alex interjected.

"No, the other one. Hey, Treasure Keeper! What will you do with the monster we've captured? Do we have what we need, or is this the wrong Lugosh?"

"It is difficult to tell if this mutant was the original Lugosh," the AI admitted after a few seconds of scanning. "The infection has altered his DNA to the point where there are only traces of the original strain left. The body shape, size, and mass are about the same, so it is possible, but it is unlikely that we could cure it, even with access to the alpha strain.

“If the infection were removed, it would likely die of old age if nothing else since it, or he, is thirty years past the average life expectancy of a Dahin that has reached physical adulthood."

Chill glanced at the Over-Keeper.

"Dahin young have an unfortunately high mortality rate," he explained. "To compensate, our females give birth to clutches of eggs to allow at least three out of ten to progress past the larval state. Dahin life expectancy is an average based on those who survive this long since if the other seven were counted, our average life expectancy would be fallaciously low. As I understand it, humans had a similar problem during their early explorations of the universe since your abysmal healthcare resulted in an appallingly high infant mortality rate."

Chill shook her head and returned her attention to the screen. That discussion was pointless. "All right, so what are we looking at? Does this fucker carry the alpha strain, or do we need to find another one?"

"My scans have detected a strain of the virus that is more advanced than those in the rest of the mutants. It fits the biological markers for the cure, so it should work."

"Fantastic." Chill nodded and tried to feel more excited. "You can make the antidote. We’ll go help our comrades fight."

"That's not how it's going to work," Ivan countered. "Not with our luck."

"Have faith," Kortez insisted. "We need to get out of

here. I won't let Zichix stick around, not if it means him getting attacked again."

Ivan reminded him, "Wherever we go, we will end up meeting someone who'll want to hurt us. Every fucking time."

Chill smirked at her team, then peered at a new scan on the screen. "There's something wrong," she stated. "There are bits of the original alpha strain and some of the original DNA. But look at that."

She knew enough about coding in general to see an error in genetic coding. There was a break in the pattern, the kind that came from repeated copying.

"Allele decay," the Treasure Keeper commented. It compared the original to the mistakes. "Errors introduced into the genome. How could there be copying errors if we're dealing with the original Lugosh?"

Chill shook her head. "I've seen this before. You get this problem when you clone from limited genetic material. Eventually, you run out of original material. Then you have to copy from the clones, and eventually, you get sequencing errors."

"Moving past why Chill knows anything about the problems cloners face," Ivan cut in, "that means this isn't the original Lugosh? That's what you're saying?"

Chill nodded. "This is eight or nine generations removed from the original. It's good work, mind you, but eventually, you get diminishing returns."

They all reached the same conclusion immediately. Chill activated the comm and hissed, "Dorian, connect me to Shoviil. Right fucking now."

"Something wrong?" he asked. "And I'm already on it. I'm getting interference on the line. Give me a second."

"Damn straight, there's something wrong," she whispered, motioning for Kortez to put his helmet back on. She didn't want them to be caught by surprise if an attack came their way. "Dorian, get it done now!"

"Working on it."

It was a trap; she knew it. The mutants were ready for them, just waiting for them to lower their guard before they attacked.

"Shoviil is on the line," Dorian announced. "Connecting you."

"What's happening?" Shoviil asked. "We've been pushing hard and going too fast for the bastards to keep up with us. Nothing's going to stop us."

"There's something wrong!" Chill cut in before he could boast further about how well his people were doing. "You are walking into a trap. Tell them to set themselves up to defend the positions they've taken and get ready for a counterattack."

"What? How do you know?"

"We got our hands on new data. Hold your fucking positions."

She would trust her instincts, especially in this situation. Her gut was telling her that they were walking into a trap that would cost them everything they had fought for.

But if the mercs, the deckies, and the Janissaries firmed up their defenses, she would bet on them against the mutants.

"Oh, shit," Shoviil whispered. "Getting reports across the board that the mutants are attacking in numbers.

They're being led by one hell of a ferocious commander. How...how the hell did you know?"

"Never mind how. Just get your people to set up defenses," Chill growled and glanced at the creature in the cell. Its calm gaze screamed that everything was wrong.

She didn't know what was coming next, but she continued, "If they can't find defensible positions, they should pull back. This effort isn't worth their lives!"

She wasn't sure if Shoviil would relay the order. Even if he did, the troops might not follow it. They were good fighters, but they were headstrong and had just the right amount of stubbornness for most circumstances.

Still, Chill had relayed the orders that would save their lives. It was up to them to follow them.

She drew her knife and looked at the monster, who was now gazing at her. "That can't be all this is. No point in letting us catch this one unless there was something inside this antechamber. Something that would have been denied him otherwise. Nothing's going to work the way we want it to, but the fighting isn't going to get it what it wants."

"What do you think we should do?" Kortez asked, hefting Cortador. "Been meaning to get some of my own back on the bastard."

"We cannot kill him," the Over-Keeper growled, stepping between her and the cell before Chill could move closer. "We need him alive to retrieve the alpha variant. The cure!"

"It knows what we're looking for," Chill answered, pointing her knife at the mutant. "They have a plan, and we're wandering right into it. We have to abort."

"Over-Keeper," Kharkanaw called on the comm. "The

beasts are gearing up for another attack. Much bigger this time."

"Are the turrets back up and running?" Chill asked. She didn't trust Kuzratha to keep the lives of his men in mind while he pursued his destiny. That was the problem with becoming emotionally invested. People got themselves into positions they couldn't get out of.

"Most of them, but I don't think it'll be enough. We might have to blow the entrances. We can survive the vacuum for a while, and you'll be safe inside the antechamber."

"Get the explosives ready," Chill answered. "We can't lose this antechamber, no matter the cost."

"Understood."

The Over-Keeper glared at her after Kharkanaw signed off. "Are you giving my men orders now?"

"Since you're failing to do so, I have to take up the slack," Chill answered. "Feel free to countermand what I said. Your Janissaries will follow your orders. However, you need to stop thinking like an intelligence operative and start thinking like someone in the middle of a war.

"That's what's happening here. It's a fucking war. Get with the program."

She shook her head. She didn't want to think about what would happen if they failed, and failure awaited them if they made the wrong play. Right now, they didn't know how it would come at them. That called for defensive action, or at least a defensive attitude.

"What would a warrior do in this situation?" Kuzratha asked. "Kill our one chance at finding a cure?"

"We now know that's not the only Lugosh clone," Chill

reminded him. "And this one is in the fucking middle of the one point on this station we can't afford to lose. If this is a trap, I want to make sure it can't do anything to jeopardize our position."

He watched her carefully. He was trying to decide if he could trust her. They'd been working together for a while, but it was still a question for him. Then he nodded.

"Keep as much of the body as intact as you can," he muttered. "Even with it dead, we'll probably be...able..."

His voice trailed off as he glanced at the cell again, trying to understand what he was looking at. Chill turned as well and saw the same look that they'd been getting from it while it was in the cell. Since most of its face was covered with greenery, it was hard to make out, but it was there.

Intelligence shone from eyes that had only reflected rage or apathy before that moment. Chill wasn't sure where it was coming from or how they could make it stop.

That was all she wanted to do now. Its lips curled up in a sentient smile like it understood what they were saying, and it took a deliberate step forward, careful not to fall over since its legs were still hamstrung.

Chill had no idea how something lacking both arms could look menacing, but she reached for her rifle. It had to die. They would have to find another mutant if they needed a live sample.

Its eyes shifted upward, and it let out a rumbling moan.

"They're attacking!" Kharkanaw announced on the comm. "They're coming in hot, too!"

"We've got attacks coming in from all sides!" Shoviil

chimed in, sounding panicked. "Pull back to defensive positions! Now, damn it! *Now!*"

Chill approached the panel, ready to open the door for some one-on-one time with the mutant. Then the lights in the room flashed red.

"Master Override accepted," the Treasure Keeper announced, a glitch marring its holographic image. "Opening the gates now."

"Say *what?*" Kortez hissed.

The answer came in a quarter of a second later when the magnetic locks on the door lifted and it silently slid open. Chill's eyes widened and she tried to bring her weapons to bear on the mutant, but it lunged forward with more power than she would have given it credit for. It brushed her knife aside and drove her rifle up as she yanked the trigger. The round hit the ceiling as she hit the deck, her breath knocked out of her.

She was relieved to see that Kortez and Ivan had been knocked over too. Otherwise, she wouldn't have heard the end of having been tackled by a hamstrung mutant with no arms. Chill realized what Lugosh, or his clone, was targeting inside the antechamber.

Kuzratha backed away as the mutant charged him. Considering the ease with which it had knocked them over —even given their surprise, they should have reacted faster —she was not shocked to see it pin Kuzratha to the deck.

The beast gurgled, and as Chill scrambled to her feet, something thick and milky-green gushed from its mouth and nose and hit the face of the Over-Keeper.

They'd seen horrible things in their day, but that took the cake. They had to put an end to whatever was happening. She raised her rifle and pulled the trigger. The first round punched through the mutant's chest and knocked it off the Over-Keeper's body. She sank her boot into its skull with a crunch and continued shooting, leaving the clone in a pile of mush on the deck.

The bastard kept smiling at her as she backed away. Kuzratha was spluttering, coughing, and trying to wipe off the muck.

"Are you all right?" Ivan asked, approaching him.

"Do…do I fucking look all right?" Kuzratha roared.

"Be advised that Over-Keeper Kuzratha has been exposed to the infection," the Treasure Keeper announced. "He must be removed from the antechamber."

"Sounds like our buddy is back," Ivan growled. "How the fuck could Lugosh take control of him in his mutated state?"

"That is a good question," the AI answered. "It might be that even in his reduced state, he programmed failsafes into me that would allow him to control me no matter what condition he was in."

"We need to rip those the hell out of you right now," Kortez stated. "Don't need you taking orders from the clones when they pop up."

"That is unlikely, but it would be prudent to clear my core code."

"We'll get right on it," Chill interjected. "In the meantime, what the hell are we looking at?"

The Over-Keeper glanced around. As much as Chill hated to believe it, he was infected. The mutant had deliberately infected him, implementing an incredibly convoluted plan to take down the leader of their group.

"We don't have much choice," Kortez interjected. "He's infected, so he's going to be a problem for us all."

"I hope you aren't suggesting that you kill me," Kuzratha growled, wiping the last of the goop off his face.

"That would be the first possibility, but no." Chill shook her head. "We need you alive to deal with the Jindahin. On the other hand, we can't just let you wander around while you're infected. We'd be making the same mistake Lugosh's crew did by letting him stay in power as his mind deteriorated. They had more reason to believe their captain would be okay, considering they didn't know what the problem was or what the infection would do.

"I believe I have a solution," the Treasure Keeper commented as they considered their options. "It was considered back in the day, but Lugosh disregarded it. The cell we put the Lugosh clone in has an isolation container as well as a cryostasis function that might slow or even halt the spread of the infection in his body as well as protect the rest of you."

"Right." She scowled. "And what should we do if you're still under the command of the clone and let him loose the moment we turn our backs?"

It was a good point. The AI had not considered the possibility prior to her mentioning it. They were now looking at an employer who was infected and desperately needed a cure—assuming one was possible.

"I don't know how I can assuage your fears on the matter," the Treasure Keeper finally answered. "I understand you have some talent in computer engineering. Can you ensure that nothing remains that would allow the infected clones to gain access again?"

Chill shrugged. "We were going to do that anyway. How do we trigger the cryostasis to keep our friend here from joining the monsters we're fighting?"

"Just put him into the chamber. I'll do the rest."

"Just put him in," the Over-Keeper muttered, rolling his eyes. "Not like I have any agency in this decision."

Chill tilted her head. "Well, it's ultimately your decision. Do you want to be cured or succumb to the infection?"

She knew what his answer would be. He'd hate it, but he didn't want his body to be subjected to the infection.

"Fine," he hissed between his teeth, then walked into the cell. "What happens next?"

"You need to lie down on the cot in the corner." The Treasure Keeper went into the cell and indicated a bed Chill had assumed was for the comfort of the inmate. However, after the Over-Keeper laid down on it, a cover slid over it. A few seconds later, the temperature in the room dropped. The glass door displayed his vital signs, which had the proper markers for a Dahin in suspended animation.

That wasn't the correct term anymore, but it was interesting to watch.

"What happens next?" Chill asked as she locked the AI out of the functions of the cell aside from maintaining the cryostasis. Even if it woke the Over-Keeper, the door would have to be opened manually.

"We need to go see if Kharkanaw needs help," Chill growled, rolling her shoulders. "After that's done, we can figure out what happens next."

CHAPTER TWELVE

Chill wondered if leaving the antechamber was the right move as the doors closed behind them. They couldn't back out now, though.

Odd how that worked out.

"Are you sure we're doing the right thing?" Kortez asked.

"Well, the door's sealed, and the Treasure Keeper will only open the doors for us, and only if the antechamber is vacant," Chill answered. She drew her rifle and checked it.

"I meant that we should let the turrets deal with the monsters and seal ourselves in there," Kortez explained. "Let the fuckers work their way through the firing corridor."

"Yeah, try talking the fucking Janissaries out of a fight for the ages," Chill muttered. "Good luck with that. You'd be lucky if they didn't declare you an enemy and gun you down."

She was kidding about them killing Kortez. From what she knew of the Janissaries, they would fight the battle even if they were locked out of the antechamber. They wouldn't turn their backs on a perfectly good fight just because it was the smart thing to do.

She wanted to think they would fight with her crew, not only because it would improve their odds when the Jindahin arrived but also because Chill felt the need to prove herself in combat when they were involved. Representing humanity seemed important. It was an ego boost, if she was honest.

It wasn't a good reason for her to put her team in danger, though.

"Nothing better than threats to get us working together with the bastards," Ivan muttered as the door sealed behind them. "I doubt they'll kill us, but it wouldn't be a terrible idea for them to think of us as being on their side. Might prove beneficial in the future."

Chill blinked. It wasn't often that she and her team were on the same page. Had they been around each other for so long that they were coming to the same conclusions? They weren't going to be on the same page every time, but hopefully, it would reduce the number of adverse discussions.

The decision had been made, so they went to fight with the Janissaries.

They didn't have far to go. Chill could already hear the sounds of the fighting, not only the rifle fire and explosions of tactical ordnance but also the roaring and groaning of the mutants. It was hard to join a fight in progress, but Chill was more than willing to rush in and find a point to attack from.

It was going much worse than they'd thought. The surge of greenery into an area that had previously been cleared had been the first and very obvious indicator of how hard the mutants were willing to push to retake the area. Behind that, a mass of creatures was pushing in. Whatever their estimate of the numbers had been, she doubled it based on the number involved in the attack on the antechamber.

Shoviil and Dorian reported that hundreds had crawled out of the prefab walls around the station and were attacking the rest of the teams. They had truly poked the hornet nest.

The clearest indicator that they were dealing with the brunt of the attack was the arrival of another deteriorated clone.

It occurred to her that if they found the part of the station where the mutants created the clones, they could remove the remaining tissue that was being used to create them. It did beg the question of why there were so many. There had to have been generations of them for the decay to have gotten to that point.

Then again, the mutants had been fighting the Scourge as long as everyone else or even longer. The clones would have fought, died, and been brought back to life over and over.

If there still was a Lugosh in the mix, his mind had probably long since broken under the pressure, leaving behind only what the mutants needed from him—a leader and a fighter.

She realized what they had to do next. The turrets were down again, taken over by the monsters. The mercs and the Janissaries had taken heavy losses and been forced back farther than they had planned.

Chill wanted to give them options.

"We need to retake the turrets," she announced, marking the points. "Why are they still down?"

"Looks like the circuits overloaded," Dorian called back. "The green stuff growing everywhere exposed the electrics. You're going to need to clear that out before they can be activated."

"Then that's what we'll do." She opened fire on the creatures that were trying to dogpile the Janissaries. Given their crude weapons and armor, it was the only way for them to win against the firepower the Janissaries had brought to bear.

Terrifyingly, it might work. There were enough to swarm whatever got in their way. Chill almost reconsidered her plan to get the turrets up and working again.

They were committed, though. They either had to keep pushing or join the defensive effort. There was no third option. None she was willing to accept, anyway.

"We're bringing those turrets back up!" she declared, opening fire on the flanks of one of the mutant waves to weaken them before they engaged the Janissaries. "We have to get them back in play. Ivan, clear us a path."

Her crewmate nodded, but he didn't look confident in his ability to do so. The deck was seething with monsters, making it difficult to see individuals, but Chill was confident in her ability to plow through them. Ivan was a lot better than he gave himself credit for, and they would keep on pushing until they could clear out the greenery.

Having confidence in her people was easy, considering their track record. Ivan had produced grenades and tossed a handful into the thick of the monsters. Chill flicked her hammer out, using it instead of her knife. She kept her rifle in her left hand and kept firing into the wall of mutants they were pushing through as she crushed bones with the hammer.

They didn't have to be thorough about killing every monster they ran into, only enough to force their way through the ones that remained.

Her poor aim didn't matter since it was a target-rich environment and every round hit a mutant. Chill threw some grenades, then opened fire again.

Next to her, Kortez had rifles in both hands. He was yelling one of his battle slogans. From nearby, Ivan was throwing knives. Chill was surprised when the knives exploded on contact and blew chunks out of their enemies before he pulled them back with the magnetic grasps in his gloves.

A lot of tech had gone into making those gloves. Chill didn't entirely understand how they worked, but work they did. Even more interesting were the new explosive blades. Each knife had to be loaded manually, so after the first explosion, it was just a knife. He couldn't reload in battle.

After the first volley of explosives had been deployed, he reverted to his rifles and cleared a path for Kortez and Chill to rush through the fighting. It would have been easier to punch through from the side, but the mutants could just turn around and attack them again.

Chill twisted and smashed the head off of the nearest creatures and forced her shoulder through the bodies of two smaller mutants on the follow-through. They were neither human nor Dahin, although she couldn't tell much beyond that. She wanted to get the outer turrets up and running, but eventually, they would have to fall back to the inner chamber. The heaviest turrets had been positioned there.

They were holding off on that since it was their last line of defense. Once they retreated, there was nowhere else to go. Oh, they could walk away from the fight and leave the vault to the monsters, but the Janissaries would not do that, and her team wouldn't leave their comrades behind.

"Ivan!" Chill shouted, indicating an approach for the group as something hammered her side. A human mutant was slamming a club into her hip, sending a tweak of pain across her body. She smashed the butt of her rifle into its head, crushing the skull, and the creature staggered back into its comrades, helpfully bunching them up to be mowed down as explosives went off behind them.

"Working on it!" Ivan shouted. He was positioning a collection of explosives pointing outward, all triggered by movement.

It was an ingenious solution, but she wanted him to help her clear out the greenery. Considering he had more knives than her, it seemed like the best choice, but since he and Kortez were defending, she would clear the infestation by herself.

"Gimme," she growled and grabbed one of the smaller

knives from Ivan's baldric, feeling a magnetic yank from the handle.

"Not that one," Ivan hissed, tugging it back. "Still got a surprise attached to it. This one."

He handed her one that didn't have explosives on it, and Chill moved over to the area where the turrets were overgrown.

Dorian called her on the comm. "You'll have to tear that shit out, then give the turrets a spark. From there, the repair functions will kick in. That said, you might want to clear the area after the repairs are done."

That told her all was not going according to plan, but it fit the kind of day they were having. Chill kept shooting with her left hand, giving Kortez and Ivan cover while ripping out the thick vines growing out of the steel and prefab.

"You need to work faster!" Kortez shouted. "Faster would be better!"

"I'm working on it!" Chill snarled. "Just, there's lots of shit around. There we go!"

She sent some power from her suit into the first receptor she found, and the electronics on the turret whirred. The monsters rushed toward where they were working.

They didn't have much time. Chill quickly moved to the next one, which was less enveloped in greenery. It had taken more damage than the first, so it required a couple of jolts from her battery to get it going.

She saw that the power shared between the turrets had kicked the others into gear, and they all opened fire on the creatures with dull roars.

"They're all online!" Dorian cackled. "You guys need to get the fuck out of there right now."

Chill narrowed her eyes. "Why? We just got a massive addition to our fi... Oh."

Another Lugosh clone was standing across from them. There were too many creepers between it and the turrets for them to shoot it.

Behind it, thousands of mutants rose in waves from the depths of the station. These were probably the people who had been on the station when the infection started. There had been millions at the time, but unlike the Scourge, the mutants couldn't piece their dead together after a battle and throw them back in. There was a hard limit on their numbers.

They could do nothing against the new assault, not even with the turrets on their side. The turrets in the inner chambers could turn those in bunches into a pile of mush. She didn't know what kind of damage those plasma cannons could do.

"The turrets will cover our retreat," Chill told Kharkanaw over the comm. "We need to fall back to the inner chamber and hope we can set up a decent defensive position before these go down."

"Agreed." Kharkanaw motioned for his team and the mercs to head out. The area had been cleared, which made it easier for them to retreat. It wouldn't take long for the monsters to break through, though, so they needed to set up their last line of defense.

Chill and the rest of the defenders fell back to get to the plasma cannons.

"A good day," Kharkanaw cackled as they approached a field aid station.

"A good day?" Chill asked. "I am surprisingly not holding a cold beverage or standing on a beach."

That got another laugh from the Janissaries' leader. "It's a good day to have so many enemies to kill. We have all the ammo we need, and we'll kill enough to pave our way into the next life."

"You believe that, don't you?" Chill smiled and shook her head. "In that context, it *is* a good day. Take away the possibility of being ripped to pieces by the dull, primitive knives and clubs they're wielding, and it's just the kind of day to celebrate."

"That is one way for it to go poorly," Kharkanaw commented with a shrug. "What a way to ruin a perfectly good battle to the death."

Kortez nodded. "I think it's pretty good. I will have a great time mashing the fuckers into paste, and it's only partly because they injured Zichix."

The turrets in the other chamber stopped shooting one by one, so they had a warning as to what would come for them through the doors they'd sealed.

"Fun times are being had by all," Chill muttered, rolling her shoulders and checking her weapons and armor. There were nicks and bumps all over both, which spoke to how close she had been to dying. If they hadn't been wearing their suits, the battle would have gone much worse for all of them.

Things might still go considerably worse for them. The plasma cannon turrets should melt through almost anything, but they had to be handled with more care than any of their other weapons. If they didn't use the weapons correctly, they could end up venting the whole damn room. One misplaced shot, and the bolts would melt through the bulkheads and expose them all to vacuum.

It wasn't the worst idea, and Kharkanaw probably already had it in mind. That would deal with most of the monsters attacking them and clear the mutants from this part of the station. Not in the long-term, but they weren't going to be dealing with the station in the long term anyway.

The turrets in the other chamber stopped shooting, and there was relative silence.

"That's all the time we got," Chill whispered, motioning for her people to join the other crews. They were setting up kill zones for anything that got past the cannons, which were powered and controlled by the AI inside the chamber.

The Lugosh clone might be able to growl a command and shut the turrets down, so they had to establish overlapping firing lines to make it through the next few hours of fighting.

"I have an idea for how we can stop the attack once and for all," Kharkanaw announced, drawing his rifle and opening fire on a pair of mutants who had climbed into their chamber through the vents.

"I'm all ears," Chill answered, scanning the crews. "Fuck it. All of us are all ears. What do you have in mind?"

"Those fuckers are being led by the mutant in charge, right?" The Janissary looked around, evincing what Chill could only describe as reticence. "Seems like if we could get to him and down him before he can head out, the rest will collapse."

"We don't know that," Kortez countered. "Maybe killing the leader will make them pissier, and we end up fighting through the death throes of these shitheads."

"It's possible, but they'll be disorganized, from what we understand," Ivan commented. "Nothing we can't handle." Kharkanaw tapped his rifle, trying to figure out how they were going to draw the commander in.

"Shit," Ivan hissed. "You want us to turn the turrets off, don't you?"

"That was what came to mind, but we can't risk it." The Janissary shook his head. "Our mission parameters stand. I'm just trying to find a way to make the fighting safer for us."

"If we had Dorian on our side, he could use a trick shot to kill the fucker," Kortez commented.

"We're not bringing him into the middle of a fight like this." Chill turned her attention to the doors, which were being pried open. A horde of the mutants was already pouring through, with nothing to stop them except for the barrage picking them apart. "Besides, I doubt we could convince him to leave the ship."

"Damn straight," Dorian muttered through the comm. "Sorry."

The apology wasn't necessary. There *was* something to what the Janissary said about being warriors and looking forward to intense fighting. The fight wasn't the point. They were heading into the battle, and she was calm, almost serene. Chill had thought that came from being used to fighting, but she'd seen people break under the pressure.

It was about their willingness to fight. She, Ivan, and

Kortez had broken personalities that let them rush into a fight without knowing how they would get back out. They wanted to survive, but they could not walk away.

Dorian wasn't broken in the same way. Oh, he was broken in plenty of other ways. Being broken was a requirement to be a member of their crew. She wouldn't judge. They all had to do what they had to do, and she would not question it.

"There are a lot of the fuckers," Chill whispered as the doors bent under the weight of the creatures assaulting them. When they cracked open and a few spilled through, they weren't satisfied but redoubled their efforts until she had to wonder how strong the mutants were.

Then again, they had just seen one of the cloned mutants power past three humans in mech armor. They didn't know what the mutants were capable of, especially in the numbers they were seeing.

"By the Rook," she heard one of the Janissaries say, gesturing. Chill assumed the movement had religious significance since the Janissaries took that seriously.

They could use help now, no matter where it came from. She raised her rifle and waited. The doors held for a few more seconds, then a loud bang echoed through the chamber. A massive bar, bent and twisted, came through the prefab and clattered on the deck, quickly followed by the doors.

Those were trampled by a wave of creepers.

Nobody had to be told to open fire. The display only stunned them for a moment before everyone fired at the creatures rushing toward them. A handful of rockets burst out of the Janissary line, along with grenades and drones, but none of them slowed the horde.

Groups of mutants went down here and there, and the ones behind them ran over the bodies of the dead and trampled the injured as they rushed in to attack.

But they didn't move directly toward the troops. Instead, the waves headed for the walls and tried to climb them to get to the turrets, which had been mounted up high, where they would be more difficult to access.

"I have a plan," Chill whispered.

Kharkanaw grinned, rows of teeth gleaming through his faceplate. "I know what you're thinking."

It wasn't a good plan. As the cannons went off, it became evident that they were the best way to thin out the mutants, but that wouldn't do the trick. With the monsters focusing on the cannons, they would eventually go down, and there would still be more than enough of the creatures left over to kill them all.

"Fuck me! You're going to let them attack the cannons, aren't you?" Kortez shook his head.

"Damn straight." She grinned like a maniac, although her faceplate wasn't transparent. It was their best play, and they all knew it. "Cover us!"

As orders went, that was as simple as could be. It didn't mean it would be easy to execute. Kharkanaw was issuing orders to his people to do the same. Since they weren't yet the focus of the attack, they could spare the firepower to clear a path for a strike team to push into the middle of the attack—where Lugosh was waiting for them.

Chill amended her previous thought. This was the

worst plan she'd ever come up with, and it would be used in one of the worst situations they'd ever been in.

"If you think we're going to stand here and watch you charge into the middle of that mess, you're fucking nuts," Ivan interjected as he fell into step beside her.

"What he said, but throw in a couple more obscenities," Kortez chimed in.

Chill looked at the pair flanking her. "I appreciate it, but I didn't want to speak for you."

Ivan snorted. "Fuck that. You wanted all the glory for yourself in the vids."

"Not cool, Chill." Kortez shook his head. "Not cool."

"Whatever. You want to join me in a suicide run to kill the bastard, you can come."

They weren't going to let her forget her selfishness anytime soon. That was fine, but if they went into the thick of it, chances were that neither of them would have the opportunity to mock her for it.

"Let's get going. No time to talk about it," Kharkanaw declared, gesturing for them to go forward. Two of the Janissaries joined him, but the rest stayed to clear a path for the strike team.

If they'd talked about what they were going to do, they would have found a reason not to. They would be going into the thick of the mutants while their plasma cannons were firing, then come to a dead halt.

Good thing they hadn't talked about it. They didn't even think about it as they surged forward.

The mutants didn't respond to being attacked from the side. Either they were too focused on attacking the cannons, or it was a matter of focusing their efforts. They probably hadn't thought anyone would charge into the teeth of their horde.

In any other situation, they would have been right.

The creepers didn't even realize they were taking fire since the cannons were still the focus of their attack. The Lugosh clone was directing the mutants, barking orders in their unintelligible language. It hadn't noticed their attack either.

Chill ducked under a wild swing at her head and bulled through a line of the creatures. She expected to have a club swing at her neck or back as she passed, but nothing came. She turned to see Kortez and Ivan covering her back, keeping the mass at bay with their melee weapons and their rifles.

"I've got a shot!" Kharkanaw declared, rushing ahead of his men.

One of the plasma cannons had hit the deck ahead of them and the beasts had scattered, which gave them an opening. It wouldn't last long, and she doubted they could make a quick retreat.

He would expect them to open a route for him to retreat through when he was done, assuming he was thinking that far ahead. Getting the job done was his sole focus, and the two Janissaries with him followed him.

Chill didn't think. Thinking would get in the way of what she was doing as she rushed in behind them, steadily firing at the creatures coming in from the left as she hacked at the ones on the right. The cannons poured rounds into the area, and their comrades kept up a barrage of cover fire. It was barely enough to keep them from being overrun.

It wasn't going to last, either. The first of the cannons hit the deck, and the creepers who managed to reach it hacked and tore at the wiring until it powered down, then moved on to the next one.

Not much could stop Kharkanaw when he built up a full head of steam. He crushed more of the creepers underfoot than shot or slashed them as he rushed toward the small open area that surrounded the clone. The larger and more powerful of the creepers tried to get in his way or at least slow him down, but three were killed in less than a second. One was run over, and another's head rolled across the deck meters away, removed with a single hack.

The third didn't have much skull left after Kharkanaw shoved his rifle into its mouth and pulled the trigger.

Janissaries were fast and deadly. Chill made a mental note to practice those tricks as she watched him face off against the clone.

Kharkanaw growled as he steeled himself for the fight. He knew about the clone's strength because Chill had both told him and had shown him recordings of what they could do, but nothing that could have prepared him for what he would meet. He could only experience it firsthand.

The clone surged forward and hammered on the Janissary's heavy armor, forcing Kharkanaw back step by step. The creatures around them wanted to join the fight, but none were allowed to. They scrambled to get out of the way to avoid being killed by their leader.

It wasn't the kind of fighting Chill was used to, but she could adapt. She tossed a grenade into the nearest cluster, easily clearing out a good number of them.

It was best to put a large number of creepers out of the fight.

After she ran out of grenades, she started shooting. Kharkanaw finally managed to regain his balance and rained strikes down on the clone, who had armor bolted to its flesh. Each strike left a dent, but the clone got in a few strikes as well.

One of the Janissaries was down. Chill hadn't noticed, but he was dragging himself clear of the creepers who were tearing at his armor and beating at the softer insides. He was still alive, but there was blood leaking out of the holes in his suit.

The other fired at the clone. Chill assumed he wasn't shooting at the head or the other vital body parts because those were tangled up with Kharkanaw.

It was enough to distract the creature, who was giving the leader of the Janissaries a great deal of trouble. He'd lost his grip on his rifle, and the mutant had gotten its hands on his knife. They were fighting for control of the weapon.

She'd never seen anything biological hold its own against mechanized armor. Well, those rock monsters they'd dealt with on Mugh-9 had, but she didn't count those. The clone was holding its own and fighting back.

The clone's orders were apparently confusing. Some of the creepers were standing around like they'd been told to do nothing. Most kept attacking the cannons.

Ivan was setting mines up to stop more creepers from coming in to join the fight. The ones that were just standing around would be dealt with eventually, but for the moment, he had larger concerns.

Kharkanaw was hammering his fist into the creature, forcing it back step by step, breaking bones and whatever was inside while they fought for control of the knife. Chill took a step forward, intending to help him, but Kharkanaw lost control of the mutant's arm. In the blink of an eye the clone drove the knife between the plates of his armor and sank it to the hilt.

The massive Dahin stopped breathing for a moment, but to his credit, he kept fighting. He grabbed the mutant's shoulder with one arm and braced its elbow with the other. No, not bracing, pushing it as he wrenched the mutant's arm into the open and brought his hand down on the elbow.

The snap was a lot louder than Chill expected, but Kharkanaw's blow had broken bone, sinew, muscle, and everything else. The commander yanked the arm out of the socket.

She knew that wouldn't be the end of the clone, but the Janissary wasn't finished. He yanked the knife out of his torso and attacked Lugosh before it could react. One stroke sent the head across the deck as the body slumped.

The creepers stopped their attack and looked at the deck where Kharkanaw was standing. The massive Janissary was still on his feet, but blood was flowing freely from his wound. There was still fight left in him, and for a moment, it seemed like the creepers would kill him and the rest of the strike team.

Then they scrambled to get away. It was like a spell had been broken. The team continued firing, but the creepers were slipping out through the vents and the doors.

Chill couldn't bring herself to shoot them. Their flight brought to mind the sentients they used to be. When they weren't viciously attacking her, Chill struggled with the same problems she'd dealt with when fighting the Bugz after she realized they weren't dealing with mindless insectoids.

Some people said all living creatures had rights, regardless of whether they were sentient, but there was more of a philosophical impact when dealing with creatures who were capable of calculus.

Still, they had bigger concerns. As the fighting wound down, Kharkanaw dropped down to his knees, releasing his grip on the knife.

"You all right there, buddy?" Chill approached, stooping to get a good look at the damage.

Kharkanaw cackled as he pulled his helmet off. "Think I should have left the knife in where it was. Got the bastard good, didn't I?"

"That you did." She didn't like his despondent tone. On top of the wound, something else was wrong. "Let's get that armor off and see about stitching you up."

"No need for that. Suit's got diagnostics." He sighed and sat on the deck instead of kneeling. That seemed more comfortable, although it didn't slow the bleeding. "Lucky stab, or he knew what he was doing. He caught me right in the *glu'bark*. No recovering from that, so I pulled the knife out and took that shit down with me."

Chill tilted her head. "Glue-what?"

"*Glu'bark*. The equivalent would be a human's aorta, although mixed in with the heart since it pumps blood too. Never mind." He shook his head, grinning and showing off those rows of sharp teeth. "Doesn't matter. Point is, I'm done for."

"Don't talk like that," Chill growled, putting pressure on the wound through the armor.

"That won't help. I'm bleeding out. Only reason I'm still here is that the suit is keeping me as alive as I can be until my heart stops beating."

He wasn't making sense, but she didn't bring that up. Chill nodded and patted him on the shoulder as she took her helmet off.

"I'm not great at reading human expressions, but it looks like you're...concerned? Or dealing with injuries yourself?"

Chill looked down at her own body to make sure she hadn't taken any damage. A few points in her armor looked like they needed repairs, but there was no severe damage. Nothing for her to worry about, anyway.

"Not injured," she answered. "Just concerned for your well-being."

Kharkanaw laughed, then coughed. "Nothing to be concerned about. A warrior's death is everything I've ever wanted. Against a worthy foe as well, and in the service of a worthy cause, to top it off. Nothing could be better for me. My battle has come to a mighty end."

The creepers had vanished.

"Well." Chill cleared her throat and nodded. "Call me selfish, but I am sorrowful about losing you as a comrade. And a friend."

"Ah. That makes sense."

She smiled as his eyes lost focus. The rest of the Janissaries had gathered around them, showing no emotion but waiting in somber silence as their leader died.

One moment, his face was serene—he was probably swimming in painkillers—and then it went slack.

"Give them hell in whatever comes next, big guy," Chill whispered, reaching over to carefully close his eyes.

There wasn't anything honorable about dying in battle. She'd lost that illusion a long time ago. However, there was something to be said for honoring the dead after they passed.

The Janissaries lowered their heads and placed a hand on their chests for a moment to grieve or maybe to honor their commander. Then they went back to their work. She looked around and saw that Dorian and Zichix had joined them, having learned the fighting was over. They'd come to find out why she wasn't communicating with them.

"What's up?" Chill asked. "Any attacks on the ship?"

"Nothing's wrong," Dorian answered. "We just came to see what was going on. Nobody was answering their comm."

Chill nodded. "Sorry. Kharkanaw—"

"We saw," Zichix interrupted, keeping her from reliving the situation. "If I had gotten here earlier, I might have been able to help."

"He said the knife hit him in the glue-back."

"The *glu'bark?*"

"Yeah, that."

"Well, then all I could have done was make him comfortable." Zichix lowered his eyestalks. He was looking better, even if she could still see the stitches that were helping him heal after the attack.

"We came here to make sure everyone was all right," Dorian continued respectfully. "But the fight is still blazing on all the other fronts. They're waiting for word and orders."

Chill nodded and stood, and the remaining Janissaries came back and picked Kharkanaw's body up. "We have a more pressing issue to deal with. Zichix, we're going to need your help with this one."

CHAPTER THIRTEEN

"What happened to him?"

The AI turned to face Zichix. It seemed like the Treasure Keeper wasn't sure what he was or whether he was part of the infestation. It had current knowledge of all the species in the galaxy but not Zichix's. Chill doubted anyone in the galaxy knew much about them.

"Answer the question," Chill growled, crossing her arms. "Zichix is the most knowledgeable physician on this station. He asks a question, you answer it. End of story."

After a moment, the AI nodded its holographic head. "The being Zichix has been designated as a friendly element. If it proves otherwise, your judgment will be called into question in the future."

The AI was more hostile now. Chill wasn't sure if that meant it was still under the influence of the clone, or if it was because they didn't have a member of the Lugosh family there to deal with him.

It didn't matter. No, it did, but they could not stop to

figure it out when the rest of their people still needed their help.

The AI spoke to Zichix for the first time. "The clone of Lugosh regurgitated an unknown liquid onto the face of Over-Keeper Kuzratha, and the infection took root in his body. I was unable to contain it, so I put him in cryostasis to ensure that the infection did not corrupt his body."

Zichix didn't enter the cell, but there were ways for him to monitor what was happening with the Over-Keeper's body while he was in stasis.

"It appears that the cryostasis is keeping the infection from spreading through his body, but it has progressed. Is there an endgame to keeping him here, or are we just waiting for a cure, as we discussed?"

Zichix was getting better at the medical officer thing.

"The cure is the only way to reverse the infestation that has taken hold of his body," the Treasure Keeper answered, approaching the cell and stepping through the walls to give the cryostasis chamber a closer look. "There was no treatment to help Lugosh when he was infected, and there is no treatment to help the Over-Keeper."

Chill sighed, trying not to jump ahead of the situation. They still had the rest of the fighting to deal with, but they were here with Zichix.

"There is another problem," the AI stated after a few seconds. "Nothing would delight me more than to hand over the treasures contained within the vault, but with the infestation currently infecting the only member of Lugosh's bloodline present on the station, it is impossible for me to do so."

"Therein lies the proverbial rub," Chill muttered.

"The rub?" Kortez asked.

"The problem," she translated. "Without access to the vault, we don't have access to the...the...whatever the fuck those holy books are. Those are the only way to ensure the Jindahin don't kill us. Nothing will stop them from blowing this place to space dust, and then the treasure will be lost to us and anyone else who is interested in it. Possibly they'll take the Serpent over, but they'll screw the mercs and the deckies out of their homes."

The Treasure Keeper nodded, imitating their human gesture. "Unfortunately, that will likely be the case. I have been directed to preserve the contents of the vault at all costs, even if they are lost forever. Allowing the station to be destroyed is an acceptable end, according to my programming."

"That's not comforting," Chill whispered, crossing her arms. "Nothing's going our way."

"I guess now is not the time to remind you that not all the Verts are functional," Dorian commented. "Given the damage done in the fighting and the losses suffered by the deckies and mercs, we might not get the wormhole operational soon enough for the Jindahin fleet to pass through."

Chill turned to look at him, eyes narrowed. "Are you serious?"

Dorian scratched his cheek. "I didn't want to bring it up before. No need to affect morale and all that, but if we're going to try to control the actions of the Jindahin, it kind of lives and dies with whatever magical texts are in that vault, as well as the person who can tell the bastards we're holding them."

"Well, ain't that just fantastic." There was no telling

when the headache had started, but it was as bad as any headache had ever been for her. "Any other bad news? Are the suns starting to tear the fucking station apart, and we only have days to set everything right again?"

Her voice was off. It carried a hint of desperation. Chill bit her bottom lip and ran a finger over her cheek, touching the scar and closing her eyes to calm down. Now wasn't the time to feel anything. They were in the middle of a war, which they couldn't put on hold for her to pull herself together.

That would have to come afterward. They'd failed so far, and if she let it get to her, they would keep failing.

When she opened her eyes, everyone was looking at her. Kortez, Ivan, Zichix, the Janissaries, and even the AI were watching her like they were waiting for her to say something. Or maybe they just wanted to know that she hadn't gotten lost in her own head.

"We need to change the plan," Chill stated firmly, clearing her throat to get the lump out of it before nodding. "We can't currently hold the Serpent against the mutants or the Jindahin, whichever shows up to kill us first."

"Got something in mind?" Kortez was the first to speak up. He was apparently still willing to follow her lead.

"We have to get people off the station." Chill shrugged. "In addition to our current efforts. If all else fails, we will save as many people as want to be saved. Those who want to stick it out and fight can do it, but we're going to have to find a way to get the others out."

"That is a worthy goal," Zichix commented, looking up

from the screen on the door to the cell. "But there is something interesting here."

"Here where?" Chill countered, trying to keep the sharpness out of her voice.

"In my examinations of the Over-Keeper." The spindly alien called up a handful of scan results. "The chamber was built to hold Lugosh, and I found records created by those loyal to him in the logs. Information that wasn't necessarily entered into the Treasure Keeper's network. I think I found the notes of one of the Dahins who was working on saving Lugosh, and he was onto something. You know, before Lugosh snapped his spine and tossed him out the nearest airlock."

She blinked a few times. "Wait, it actually says—"

"I inferred some of that, but there was an immediate medical scan on the crew member after he was killed, and the spine was fractured by a powerful hand gripping and twisting it. That would indicate that Lugosh showed signs of incredible strength a lot earlier than we thought."

Zichix tilted his eyestalks like he wanted to look into what had happened but was putting it aside for the moment. "Anyway, he made a lot of progress toward a cure, but I'm going to need a few samples of the alpha strain."

"Wait, what about the ones we killed?" one of the Janissaries asked. "We have two of the clones. That should give you more than enough samples to work with."

"The samples decay quickly," the AI explained. "We might be able to dig something out of the remains, but I don't have high expectations for that."

Chill scowled. "All right, so we have to find another of

those fuckers and retrieve some live alpha strain samples for Zichix to work with."

"Where?" Ivan countered.

"That is where we're going to have to come up with a plan," Chill answered. "If you have the samples, can you cure the Over-Keeper?"

"The Over-Keeper?" Ivan asked. "Don't you think we should focus on clearing the creepers out first?"

"I don't know. That means getting to the original fucker." Chill rolled her eyes. "You know, the asshole all the other assholes came from? There has to be an original from which all the other clones are created. We get to that one, and we'll stop them from creating more clones. That will take the backbone out of their little army."

Calling it a little army when it had ripped reinforced doors out of the wall felt disingenuous, but she was pissed. She was saying things she didn't mean because of that.

"Not only that," Zichix answered, "but I believe we're looking at a very real possibility of healing those who are infected. There's no telling what kind of state those bodies will be in once the infection has been removed, of course. The damage from being infected for longer than a few months might cause the person to die, but a cure might be better than being yanked around by some bioweapon."

Chill could see that. She could also see that some people would prefer to remain infected, even if it meant being a puppet to the mutation, if they lived longer.

A lot longer, from what they now knew.

"You sure?" she asked, trying not to get her hopes up.

"As sure as I can be about anything," Zichix answered

with a gentle shrug of his spindly limbs. "Limited tests were run back in the day, and the results were hopeful."

The AI checked the data and nodded again, the motion unnatural for Dahins. "We'll only know for sure after we have an alpha strain sample to complete the sequence, but the Zichix specimen is correct."

She looked at her crew. "That means we need to get our hands on the alpha strain. There are plenty of clones killing our people out there. About time we rejoined the fighting."

Chill put her helmet back on and ran a check on her armor. There were several alerts about the state of the plates, but the mech was functional, and they didn't have time to have Ibu look at it.

"What do you need me to do?" Zichix asked.

"Keep an eye on the Over-Keeper's status and let us know if anything changes," Chill answered. "Not likely if he's in stasis, but I'm not leaving anything to chance when it comes to this fucking shit. More importantly, keep running sims to see if there's anything else we can learn from what was happening back then."

"Will do."

Kortez approached her, tapped her shoulder, and connected on a private channel. "Are you sure this is a good idea? Leaving Zichix here with an AI who might turn against us at the wrong word from one of those clones?"

"Up to you." Chill eyed Zichix carefully. "And him. In the end, we need someone who's not the AI keeping an eye on the Over-Keeper. We could leave a couple of the Janis-saries here to make sure nothing goes wrong."

He didn't look convinced, and Chill almost suggested that he stay here. She didn't want him distracted out in the field, worrying about his kid. Besides, Zichix had been through a traumatic experience. Having his dad around would reduce the stresses in the new environment.

Kortez sighed. "That sounds reasonable. We'll bring the pain to those fuckers."

"Plus, the rest of the Janissaries will hold the area outside, as well as the mercs."

"Really? We're not taking them with us?"

"We'll go reinforce our allies, but this chamber is still of vital importance. The fuckers will attack this place again. We need to get the defenses back up and make sure this area is in no danger. That means from the AI as well."

She couldn't shake the feeling that the Treasure Keeper was listening to their conversation. She'd looked into its capabilities, and everything that didn't involve keeping the vault intact was outdated by at least a decade, sometimes more. However, one never knew what they were dealing with when it came to AIs, especially those whose shackles weren't as secure as they should have been. They were known for picking up things they had no business knowing.

There was no indication that he was reacting to what was being said, but it was something to keep in mind, even if she was just being paranoid.

"You good?" Chill asked, patting Kortez's shoulder. She was careful not to cause any damage to either of their suits as she did so. "If you'd feel better sticking around here, I understand."

"Nah. Well, I *would* feel better being close to him, but I don't think I'd do any good here. Might as well join you in crushing those fucking creepers."

"Good. Let's get going."

CHAPTER FOURTEEN

There wasn't much talk on the ship. Alex was flying them to one of the Verts to join the other teams. Dorian had stuck with Zichix to keep an eye on the AI, even if he said it was so he could program in loops and defenses in case one of the clones tried to take it over again.

The AI had to permit that, considering its core programming focused on keeping it from being compromised by the mutants and the infestation. As it turned out, the clone's takeover had been a massive breach.

Dorian knew how to sweet-talk AIs. Not enough people appreciated that skill, in her opinion.

Getting back into a fighting mindset proved to be more difficult than she had anticipated. She was still stuck on what had happened to Kharkanaw. Seeing him go down had been a blow to her confidence. She wanted and indeed needed to believe they had a chance against the monsters, but seeing a Janissary go down brought up doubts she couldn't afford.

If someone like Kharkanaw had died to bring one of the

clones down with him, what chance did *they* have? The one they'd brought in had wanted to be taken captive.

If it hadn't, it would have killed Kortez when it had him in its grasp. If they ran into one of those fuckers again, she would blast its extremities to pieces before getting up close and personal. It would still be a threat, but they would have a better chance of securing it if it didn't have legs or arms.

Chill looked up from working on her suit to check on the rest of the crew. Ibu was helping Kortez fix the damage to the plate over his left thigh, and Ivan was running a whetstone over his knives. She'd seen him carefully applying explosives to them a few minutes before. He must have nerves of steel to handle the blades now.

None of them commented that she was brooding. She wasn't used to not being picked on for it, which spoke volumes about how they were feeling under the pressure of what was happening. She wasn't sure she liked it. She was supposed to worry about everything while they ribbed her good-naturedly about it. The rules of the world were hard and fast, and nothing should be able change them.

Chill wasn't going to let it stand.

"Looks like you're all taking a page out of my book," Chill growled, approaching Ivan and Kortez. "Here you all are, brooding and leaving none for me."

"Sorry, boss," Kortez answered with a small smile. "It seemed appropriate for us to follow your example."

"Well, cut it out. Worrying about all the different ways shit could go wrong is my job. It's on the lot of you to remind me that I worry too much and to stop giving myself wrinkles that'll have to be ironed out by the best plastic surgeons in the galaxy when we're all old and rich."

That got a smirk from Ivan, but Ibu just shook her head while she worked on Kortez's armor. She was the most sensible of all of them, and she knew how crazy the whole crew was. That was her job—being the sensible mother and shaking her head as they made every mistake in the book. She couldn't stop them. All she could do was put them back together when those mistakes battered them to pieces.

Their armor, at least.

"I actually had an idea," Ivan commented, changing the subject. "Not an idea, more of a hunch, really. Alex, can you connect us with Shoviil at the forward command center?"

"Connecting you now," Alex answered, her soft, soothing voice coming over the speakers.

"I wonder who it was who voiced all the AIs," Kortez muttered. "I mean, have you ever noticed that all the AIs with a voice interface have soft, feminine voice? Even the male voices. They're always this soft voice almost whispering in your ear."

"Considering the fears people have about AIs, maybe the people who create the voice interfaces don't want their clientele being yelled at in Vichian by a burly fellow."

Chill grinned. "There might be a market for that."

"But who does the voicing?" Kortez asked. "There's got to be some basis for the voices."

"Nope." Well, there is, but the original data was recorded by voice actors a hundred and fifty years ago, so nobody remembers who it was. The generic voices are tapped from those two or three dozen original voice actors. You generally get to the point where the personality of the AI determines which voice they use. You *can* get AIs with generic automated bot voices, but marketers found they didn't sell well. You pay someone famous to voice your AI for you if you like."

She thought everyone knew the history of AI development. The cast networks gave a quick recap every time there was even a hint at an uprising, but apparently, some people didn't pay attention. Maybe they didn't care.

"What's your hunch?" Chill asked to change the subject.

Ivan raised a finger to tell her he would get to that when Shoviil spoke. "Chill, Ivan, Kortez, good to find that you're still alive." The Xo sounded frazzled, but his statement was genuine. "We're in the middle of it here, so forgive me if I'm short."

"No need," Chill answered. "Ivan had an idea—"

"A hunch," Ivan corrected her.

"Whatever. Tell him what you're thinking."

"Right." Ivan cleared his throat and called up something on his HUD before speaking. "I was wondering about the life support systems on the station. You know how they have automated cleaning processes that get rid of trash and other undesirable elements that aren't caught in the atmo scrubbers? I was wondering if anyone knows who or what has access to the system panels. We could figure in what gets cleaned and what's prioritized by the systems across the station."

"Hmm." Shoviil sounded like he wasn't sure where the conversation was going but was interested in finding out. "We can access those systems from here. They're networked, but the automated systems use very complex sensors to see which areas in the Verts need cleaning and how to access them. It's one of the most complex systems I've ever seen, although that's not the highest bar."

"I don't think we have to figure it out," Ivan countered. "The Treasure Keeper has kept track of the situation since the beginning, so it knows how it all runs."

"Sure, but there are plenty of areas in the Verts where the systems have been defunct for a while. Some systems were shut down because there was no AI or VI to run them."

"He might be able to get them working again," Chill muttered. Ivan was still furiously researching to see if his idea would work.

Finally, he found what he wanted. "I'm no expert, but I'm pretty sure he can get his circuits wrapped around that sort of thing. I don't think we could get the station to treat the infestation as filth that needs to be cleaned, though."

"Yeah, I was about to say." Chill shook her head. "It would take a long time to rewrite the code, and that's assuming the inner workings don't run diagnostics and correct any changes they find."

"That would make it more complicated than what we can do. Besides, it wouldn't help us find Lugosh and the alpha strain we need. No, I was thinking we might tune in on those sensors so we can find the fucker without needing to set any traps."

Chill opened her mouth to voice her dissent, but she was surprised to find that nothing came to mind. The systems had manual ports so an admin could program bots to clear one mess before the rest. For that, they had to access the sensors, so there was already a user interface in place.

Theoretically, it was possible to access the system from the network. In practice, it would be difficult. It was all code she'd never seen before and had no experience with, which meant they would need help.

"I guess there's no reason not to see if it's possible." Chill spoke to Dorian over the comm. "Hey, we need to have a word with the Treasure Keeper if he's not busy."

"Is something wrong?" Dorian countered, sounding stressed.

"No, but there might be something we can do to make things better," she explained.

"I am at your service, Captain Chill," the AI told her.

"It's not 'captain.' We were wondering if you can access the sensors used by the cleaning processes on the station. From what we can see, those sensors would tell us where the clones are. We could track them that way."

"I see." The AI ran through the necessary checks. They could pull it off, but he needed to work through the code to find out if what they were suggesting was possible. "You might be right, although it will not be easy. Most of the sensors pick up a variety of markers, but none of them say they're looking at a creeper. I'll use the location data, size, and movement to tell us where they are."

"Are you telling me we can do it or you're already doing it?"

"Data has been gathered. Collating now. I will message you when I have results."

Kortez grinned. "I love his optimism. *When* he has results, not if."

"Uh, Chill?" Shoviil interrupted. "There's something going on here."

Chill tilted her head. He didn't sound panicked enough to tell her there was an emergency, but he did sound confused. Like he wasn't quite sure what he was looking at, but he didn't like it.

"What's going on?" She was curious and wanted to know if they needed to change their approach.

"The creepers...stopped attacking."

That didn't sound right. Chill checked the comm to make sure the pause wasn't just a chunk of the sentence dropping out, telling her that she was missing context, but no. The rest of the troops were talking about how the creepers were pulling back from the fighting even though the deckies and mercs were pushing into their territory. There was no tactical advantage to retreat since that would allow their enemies to regroup and get ready for another attack.

"Hold on," Shoviil cut in. "Looks like movement. Not enough to show an attack. One of the Lugosh clones came out in the open, and it's alone."

"Well, looks like we have an alpha strain source," Kortez growled. "Can you pounce on it before his people back him up?"

"No. It's keeping its distance, and if we attack, there's a sewer access right behind it. It'll be out of reach. Hold on. It's trying to communicate with us."

That didn't sound right either. They had never seen the creepers try to communicate with anyone except other mutants.

"Get us vid of what's going on," Chill requested, then she was inundated by communications from the rest of the teams at the front, saying they were looking at the same thing: one clone out in the open, trying to communicate.

Thankfully, one of the Janissaries at the front shared his HUD feed with the comm links. Another one started streaming as well.

The clones were waving their arms like they were trying to get the attention of the people in front of them.

After a few more minutes of waving, they got the attention they were looking for and started speaking. Not in any language she'd ever heard, though. Chill wondered if it was trying to communicate with them in the language they used to communicate with the other creepers, but after a few sentences, it was clear that they were all speaking in unison in the old Dahin tongue.

"Can anyone translate this?" Chill asked, looking around.

"Yes," the Treasure Keeper announced. "They are delivering an ultimatum. If you abandon the station, you will be spared. If you remain on the station for another day cycle, you will all be drowned in a tide of... I'm not sure what that word means, but I assume he's talking about creepers. A tide of creepers that never ends."

That was an interesting way to put it, considering that their attack on the antechamber had seemed like a wave rushing forward.

"You're connected to the sensor system now, right?" Chill closed her eyes. The clones were repeating the message to make sure that everyone understood.

"Yes."

"How capable are they of delivering on this ultimatum?"

There was a pause on the other end. The AI was still

collating the data it had collected. She assumed terabytes came into the central servers every minute, keeping the centralized brain updated on everything that needed to be cleaned up or maintained.

"I believe they can deliver on their threats," the Treasure Keeper answered. It displayed the collated data in a way they would easily understand.

The results were about what Chill was expecting. Even with their powerful attacks, the mutants were still holding back. Considering the numbers she was looking at, she couldn't figure out why. And why they were bothering with an ultimatum?

Even if she reduced the total by ten percent, there were more than enough creepers to wash them all off the face of the station without a second thought. They would have to take out sixty or seventy percent before they would have a chance.

They were looking at a full-on army in the number generally used to occupy moons, asteroids, and the odd lightly populated planet.

"Holy fuck," Kortez murmured, studying the population estimate and its distribution across the station. "I guess we know the fuckers have been very measured in their attacks on us so far."

"There's the population center right there." Ivan called up an area where bright yellow dots indicated groups of fifty had gathered. "They're not bothering with housing. Storing them like bots until they're needed. See there? That's ten per square meter."

They were all inactive, showing none of the indicators that would be picked up on life sign scans, but the new parameters didn't give them much hope that they could stand their ground against what was coming.

Once again, Chill found herself wondering why the mutants were bothering with an ultimatum. There was no reason for them to do anything but roll over anything in their way since the Scourge was gone.

"Now we know where we'll likely find the alpha strain," Ivan pointed out, ever the pragmatist.

"The deckies aren't going to walk away from the station," Chill commented. "That tightens the clock for all of us. One cycle to get the sample, or everything we've worked so hard for will be gone and a whole mess of people will be dead."

"No pressure," Kortez added.

"Would you like me to alter the course?" Alex asked through their comms.

She sighed, then nodded. "Yes, I think we have to go elsewhere."

CHAPTER FIFTEEN

They were facing overwhelming numbers. There was nothing they could do about that. In an out-and-out ground battle—or station battle, if they wanted to be semantically correct—they would lose. They had the fire-power advantage, but they couldn't do much with a couple hundred fighters against tens of thousands of mutants. Not with those creatures knowing everything there was to know about the station.

It couldn't be done. A full retreat was ordered, with all the troops at the front falling back from their attack points. Chill could only assume they were being watched by eyes they couldn't see or detect. They had to make a show of abiding by the terms of the ultimatum.

One day to leave, and everything would be fine. Stick around, and they would be massacred. Chill doubted they could put a dent in the mutants' numbers. As the game stood, they didn't stand a chance.

That made their option simple; they had to change the rules. They would have no chance if they went toe-to-toe against the mutants, so they had to head into space. They had ships; the mutants didn't. Ships that could be seen leaving the station, never to return.

It was a reasonable deal. They could clear out, leave everything behind, and let the Jindahin deal with the infestation. They would blast the station instead of committing the troops and resources required to take it back Vert by Vert. They would wreck the place and move along, returning to the war they were supposed to be winning but were really losing. Chill still couldn't wrap her head around that conundrum.

Maybe that was why the mutants wanted them to depart. It wasn't a matter of wanting to spare the intruders on their station but conserving their resources and their home for the much bigger fight that was on the way.

As Chill looked at the small fleet they had gathered around their ship, it seemed like they were going to have to make things more interesting. In the minds of the mutants, everyone who could leave had been evacuated. They were abiding by the ultimatum, so there was no reason for the mutants to prep for a fight.

That would change, but hopefully, they would have the element of surprise. With that in mind, she'd pulled everyone out of the antechamber where their resident AI was waiting. She still didn't trust it not to tell Lugosh everything it needed to know about what they were doing so it could prepare.

"I've got to say, attacking them from the outside is one of your best ideas yet," Dorian commented as he ran the required checks before they set it to combat mode. "Regardless of execution, it was a great idea. I appreciate you keeping us all three or four thousand klicks from the opening salvo a great deal too. I just have one question, though. How is what we're doing any different from what the Jindahin plan on doing?"

"Well, for one thing, we're not intentionally blowing the whole fucking station up," Chill answered.

"Intentionally or not, if we hit one wrong spot, the whole station goes up anyway."

"Right, but then we'll have the time to fuck off before the Jindahin fleet arrives and tries to sort out what happened to their beautiful station." Chill grinned. "Seems like a better idea than just waiting around for them to show up. To my mind, anyway."

"We'll probably be on the run from the Jindahin."

"We can change our names, dump the ship, and start over. It wouldn't be the first time for any of us."

She raised an eyebrow at Dorian, waiting for him to question her assumption, but nothing came. That answered the questions she had for him. He had done it before. He was on the run from something.

Chill had no interest in digging deeper. His life was his life.

"Looks like we're about ready to go," Dorian announced, activating the comm link with the rest of the ships in their little fleet. "Not exactly overwhelming fire-power. Really wish we had the Over-Keeper's ship. A lot more guns on that one."

"If that one was still working, we wouldn't have had the defenses in place to keep us alive in that last push by the fuckers," Chill reminded him. "I'll take the tradeoff. We wouldn't have been able to pull the whole ship together in the time we had, anyway. It took us eight hours to just get all the mercs, deckies, and Janissaries up on the plan. It would have taken a lot longer to put the ship back together."

"Right." Dorian scowled. "Still, I don't like the idea of leaving Zichix in the antechamber. It's not the place I want him to be if we're looking at wrecking the station with our attack. I know that's not likely, but eventually, we're going to hit something that does that if we keep causing damage, right?"

"I had Alex run simulations on how the station would collapse," Chill explained, checking the rest of the ships. "Based on the worst of the sims, it will take three hours to go critical.

"If it all goes to shit, if we're not dead, we'll have enough time—just enough—to pick Zichix up. He knows it, and if there's a problem, he knows where to go so we *can* pick him up and jump away before we get pulled into the wormhole or caught in the blast radius or whatever the hell happens when a wormhole loses the power maintaining it."

She'd read papers about that. There were a plethora of theories, and none of them made sense to her. She would have to spend three or four decades studying physics, algebra, and core mathematics to begin understanding them. Since she'd been bored to tears after three hours, further academics were not in her future.

What the experts *did* agree on was that a collapsing wormhole would not end well for anything in the area around it. That much she understood. It was simple. They didn't want to be anywhere near the station when it went up.

All the checks came in. The ships were ready for a fight. Most were civilian ships that had been illegally fitted with plasma cannons and the odd missile tube. Their 'vette had the most and biggest guns in their fleet.

"All right, everyone run a comm check," Chill called. After everyone had sent her a ping to let her know they were listening, she continued, "Keep in mind that when we start our run, the aggression is going to supersede the coding that has kept us safe from the defenses thus far. The moment we fire, the defenses will come online. Keep that in mind when plotting your course. Aside from that, remember where you're attacking and stick to your squads, and we'll get out of this alive."

She got back a chorus of "aye ayes" from the rest of the captains. It had taken a lot of plotting, planning, and maneuvering to get almost everyone on one of the ships. Most of the fighters were ready to head in. While they would have surprise on their side, they wouldn't have an easy go of it. They were looking to cause damage and make a ruckus while distracting the mutants from the real object of the mission.

Chill took a deep breath, watching and feeling their ship move through space, heading around the station and away from the reaching tendrils of the nebula as they started their run. She would man the guns while Dorian focused on flying. They'd done this before while being shot at the whole way in.

No, it wouldn't be a pleasant experience.

"Weak spots are highlighted on your screens," Chill

announced over the comm as Alex did that. "Time to start the runs. Good luck."

She was sending a lot of them to their deaths, maybe even her and her crew, but they were committed. The sensors on the station were picking up on their active plasma cannons and the targeting from the missile tubes. The turrets on the outside of the station activated and started targeting them.

"I stand by what I said." Dorian nodded. "Great plan. Regardless of how it goes, turning it around on them and forcing the mutants to fight the battle on our terms is the way to go."

"I appreciate your optimism." Chill loaded the missile tubes as the first of the turrets on the station fired at their fleet.

With Alex helping with the calculations and targeting, she just had to pick the targets to carve a path for the rest of the ships to go in. That was one of the downsides of having the ship with the most firepower. Then again, it was better that the turrets were largely aiming at them.

"First attack path opened up," she called as plasma rounds melted through the turrets and blobs of the molten steel floated into the vacuum. "Second path opened up. Nice work, Alex."

"I appreciate the positive comment, and I will attempt to maintain my efforts to optimal capacity," the AI answered.

It wasn't the answer she had expected, but Chill had turned her attention to the third avenue of approach the other ships would be using. One sweep was all they had time for, which meant that whatever turrets they couldn't crack down on would have to be handled by the mercs and the deckies.

"That's number three done," Dorian whispered as he pulled the ship away from the station to draw fire from the turrets that remained as the other ships closed in. "Now for the hard part."

"Not really." Chill scowled. They flew toward the largest concentration of creepers to damage the armor. It was the most brilliant part of their plan, she thought, and it would take some work to make it happen. "Missiles away."

The thunk of the tubes opening up indicated the missiles were away. They remained inactive for a few long seconds, propelled by the explosive decompression of the tubes suddenly being exposed to gravity. When they were too close to the station to be hit by the turrets, their thrusters activated. Their targeting chips directed them toward the point they needed to strike.

Chill loaded two more missiles and fired. The thrusters kicked in almost as soon as they were out of the tubes and quickly gained on the other two.

The plasma cannons raked fire across the hull of the station, melting through the armor over the weak point, which had been attacked by coilguns or asteroid strikes at some point in the past, and softening the targets up further. Despite the repair functions on the station, the areas were still pocked with craters to show where they needed to hit. It made everything easier.

"Come on, come on," Chill whispered as a couple of turrets swiveled around to hit the missiles and were instead hammered by rounds from their ship.

"Good hit," Dorian announced, watching the quadruple

explosion push chunks of armor in until the hull couldn't take the strain and cracked.

Physics intervened as the atmo inside the station vented, ballooning the weakened armor structure outward and tearing ship-sized chunks out. It caused a chain reaction across the other weakened points and ripped a massive hole in the station's armor.

"Bring her in," Chill called. The other ships were on their own now, leaving them the job of heading in while the rest of the teams defended themselves.

Dorian nodded and twirled the ship through space a few times before jackknifing it around. The cannons all fired, and two more missiles flew into the gap they'd created, driving the damage deeper a few seconds before they sped through the hole.

The ship rocked, shuddered, and quaked as they flew in, cannons still firing. They didn't have any missiles left, but the damage had been done.

The gravity in the Vert told her they'd ground to a halt. For a wonder, their ship was mostly intact.

"Happy landings all around," Dorian commented with a weak grin, wiping beads of sweat off his forehead.

"Yep," Chill agreed. "This is where the fun begins."

CHAPTER SIXTEEN

"Something's not right."

Those three words summarized their history as freelance mercs. At this point, if something went the way they'd planned, she would be suspicious and wait for something to pull the rug out from under their feet.

Kortez was right. Something was wrong with the situation they were in. They had blasted their way into the station, and they should have caused a lot more damage than they had. Chunks of the station should have broken free, leading to further damage as the atmo in those sections vented.

Most of the damage they were seeing had been caused by the explosions, but enough of the Vert was intact that they had crashed into one of the remaining sections and damaged the ship.

Dorian had kept the collision from doing more than dinging their armor, but the fact remained; something wasn't right.

"Reports are coming in from the other attack points,"

Dorian announced. "We lost one of the ships on the way in. All the others penetrated the defenses. They're prepping for the attack now, but they're not facing any immediate resistance."

"Of course they're not," Ivan muttered, shaking his head. "We exposed most of the Vert to vacuum, and those fuckers need a functioning, livable area to survive. Chances are we killed a few hundred of them by blowing the area up."

That had been the hope, and it was the reason they had done the damage they had. Even so, there was no guarantee that what they were doing would put a dent in the number of mutants in the station.

Still, it didn't look like the creepers were resisting. They were getting no readings from the sensors. It wouldn't last, but Chill hoped they would get a warning when danger approached.

"I hate to say it, but I kind of miss the days when the Scourge was all we were dealing with," Ivan admitted. "I'm not sure whose idea it was to come up with this sort of virus, but those assholes need to be chained up outside a barn somewhere and shot."

"There's something weird about this place," Kortez growled, pointing at various sections of the Vert they were moving through. "Those points there? They're the usual support structures we see in most of the Verts, but they've been reinforced."

"Could be it was damaged a long time ago, and they were braced to avoid that shit happening again," Chill surmised. Considering how old the station was, anything was possible.

"No, it's not that," Kortez insisted. "The scan says it's not steel, prefab, or any of the usual stuff used to shore up that kind of damage."

He was right. Chill ran scans of her own, and the structures didn't exhibit the usual markers.

"Biological material," Chill whispered, flicking on one of the headlamps on her HUD to give them a better view of the dark chamber they were entering. "I think we're looking at a fuck-ton of the creepers."

The light gave them a definitive answer. Chill didn't want to get any closer, and thankfully, their HUDs let them zoom in. The bodies of creepers were intertwined with roots. The roots acted as mortar and the bodies were the bricks.

It was unsettling. Although brain activity only showed up when the creatures were activated, the ones they were looking at were clearly dead. Even the greenery was dying, having suddenly been deprived of the atmo it required to survive and freezing thanks to the drop in temperature. The conglomeration had reinforced the area and was holding the station together.

Unfortunately, they could not tell if it had been a recent addition the mutants had put up in preparation for the attack. That would have told them Lugosh had been warned of the attack before it happened. With the damage already done and a stationary cloud of dust and soot that hadn't been yanked out with the rest into space, they didn't know if they would have an AI problem waiting for them when they got back.

"There were a bunch of them in here," Ivan noted. "You can see them floating. Well, not anymore; they flew out of here almost as fast as we flew in. Lots of dead fuckers. I'd say about the same number of assholes we cleared out in our last battle."

Chill shook her head and moved on. They had to assume those creepers were dead.

"Other teams are talking about what they're running into," Dorian called from the ship. "The station's defenses are starting to come online, but not enough of them to pose a problem. The real problem is coming from the creepers."

"Wait, what?" Chill called up the locations of the other teams as they pushed in faster than the DEMC troop. "No, that can't be right. The areas they're in should still have vacuum."

"I don't know what's going on. I'm only reporting what they're telling me."

She picked up on movement ahead of them. The lack of atmo meant everything was still moving after the explosive decompression. It was difficult to see what it was. Still, she had assumed everything would be dead until they reached the areas that still had atmo.

As they headed deeper, they saw that the movement was purposeful, not just the listless floating of materials that had been disturbed by the decomp.

Kortez growled and drew Cortador, twirling it a few times. "How the fuck are they surviving in vacuum?"

Chill thought they would find out before too long. She drew her hammer, flicked it on with one hand, and readied her rifle in the other. Ivan had chosen to fight with his rifle instead of his knives. As good as he was with either, the fluctuating grav in the Vert would be enough to throw his aim with his knives off.

They had a small horde heading their way, although they hadn't been expecting to run into resistance yet.

Chill highlighted them for the other two before guiding her group toward them. She took a deep breath to steady herself. It was odd that she wasn't feeling the effects of the altered gravity in the Vert.

Usually she would have been fighting the need to fill her suit with the compressed power bars she'd scarfed down before the space battle started, but nothing was forcing its way back up. She was either getting better or there wasn't enough of a disturbance for her body to react. Either way, she was glad none of it was going wrong. The plan depended on it.

There was something different about the creatures they were approaching. Chill noticed it when they came into view. Whatever was covering their skin made them look bigger and burlier than usual. Whatever it was could probably act like armor as well as keep them alive in the vacuum.

"Come to Papa, you little bastards!" Kortez roared, charging forward and bringing his knife around to take the head off one of them.

The strike went deep but fell short of cutting the head off. Still, it broke the seal, and the creature inside started choking in the vacuum.

That was all Chill needed to know. She jumped in and crushed the skull of the closest one as Kortez feigned a retreat. The other three fell back under a barrage of rifle fire from her and Ivan.

"That's unsettling," Kortez whispered when the small squad was dead or dying. "I mean, if they can protect their creepers from vacuum and fit them with armor to make them more resilient, why don't we see this on a lot more of them?"

Chill shrugged, managing to keep her suit from jumping with the gesture. "Might have to do with resources. Whatever's driving the mutants might not care enough about them to bother since it seems happy to let countless creepers get chewed up by our attacks."

It was a surprisingly sentient reaction. Many people said sentients wouldn't just throw their people into the shredder like these commanders had, yet the millions fighting in pointless wars or dying on far-flung asteroid mining ventures, in prison colonies, and in other horrific endeavors spoke to that being untrue.

She motioned for her team to keep moving. The Vert was still stable despite the damage they'd caused, and they were approaching the first of the areas which were sealed and still had some atmo.

The area around them changed. It took her a full minute to pick up on what it was, but finally she saw something crawl over the walls and support units.

"I guess we have our answer," Chill muttered, as she sent one round into the growth and watched it scorch its way through. The damage was immediately grown over by the greenery. "Maybe the fucking mutants didn't know they could do this kind of thing before now."

"So, our attacks have made them stronger every time?" Ivan scowled and fired a couple of times before shrugging. "We need to get the cure going before they find a way to work around that too."

He had a point. They had to formulate a plan if the

creepers had already figured a way around the cure. Considering Lugosh had been the first to know about the cure and had wanted to do away with it, that seemed likely. They could not change that, and if he knew what they were aiming for and wanted to get rid of them, he would have plenty of time to do it.

Assuming he didn't want to be cured anymore. It had been high on his priority after he was infected, and he had only put a halt to their efforts because what they were working on would likely kill him. The formula the AI was devising might leave him alive, but it might not. After so many years of being exposed, there wouldn't be much of the original Lugosh left even if they cured him.

Maybe that was why he was fighting them so hard.

"All right," Chill began as they reached a makeshift airlock. "Looks like there's atmo in the next chamber, but there have been breaches."

"Shouldn't be atmo if there were breaches," Kortez pointed out as they worked on opening the door. "And the repair functions wouldn't have kicked in until after the atmo was vented."

"Maybe they put up a particle shield," Chill surmised. "It would take a lot of power, but it would seal the place."

"Nope," Dorian countered. "We would have seen a massive uptick in energy usage in the Vert if that had been the case. More importantly, there would have to be generators set up in this area for a particle shield to even be possible. There's something else going on in there. Hell, a couple of breaches are still sucking air out, so maybe something big got sucked into the hole and it's keeping atmo inside while it's being pumped in from elsewhere."

They could surmise all day, but the only way they could answer the question was by getting the door open.

Which was a lot more difficult than it would normally be, considering the difference in pressure between the two rooms. Dorian stepped in to help seal the room on the other side of the door so it could pressurize properly and allow them through.

They stepped into a residential area with foundations for more intimate housing than in the larger complexes across the station. Nothing had been built, or if it had, everything had been torn up and nothing had replaced it. There were a handful of park areas where the children of those running the station could have fun. Complex steel climbing toys were all that was left of what it had been.

"It's weird to think people lived here once upon a time," Chill commented as the room repressurized to allow them to access the Vert without facing the same difficulties every time they wanted to open a door. "It makes me think about all the fucking monsters we've had to deal with."

Kortez chuckled. "I don't know, maybe one day people will live here again—assuming we can clear the monsters and keep the Jindahin from tearing the place apart."

Chill doubted it would happen in their lifetimes. It would take a while for people to decide they wanted to settle in the area and even longer for them to bear bunches of new sentients to populate the rest of the station. Assuming they managed to keep the station intact while clearing it, Chill thought it would be fifty years before the process reached that point.

"All right, looks like the area's pressurized and ready for

you to go through," Dorian announced as they reached the door. "Just keep moving, right, guys?"

That seemed odd, like he was trying to drive them forward.

"What's the matter, Dorian?" she asked as the door opened.

"Nothing yet, but the other teams are reporting really weird goings on in there. They don't know how to explain it, and honestly, neither do I. It's the kind of thing you have to see to believe."

That seemed like just another day on the station. As things stood, they still had two-thirds of the day Lugosh had given them left to vacate. However, she felt attacking the mutants as they had would put a damper on any possibility of a defense.

Dorian was right too. This chamber was large, and from the looks of it, that was only the start of the craziness they would be facing. The sudden decompression had caused a snap freeze, but something else was afoot. The growth was a lot more aggressive in this room, and she could see it starting to grow like a film across the whole structure, even starting to cover the breaches, sealing the breaches until the room could maintain its atmo again, although the temperature was still well below what would be considered remotely livable for organic creatures.

There was ice plastered across most of the surfaces, showing the kind of atmo that had been in the chamber before they attacked.

Even so, they were looking at more or less the same thing they'd been looking at in the previous chamber. Hundreds if not thousands of creepers were holding the chamber together despite the damage the missiles had caused.

Chill slowed down so they didn't slip on the ice as they moved forward.

"Who would have thought it?" Ivan muttered, looking around for creepers. "Freezing the shit out of the bastards kills them dead. We should have come up with a bunch of new ways to make their days miserable."

"I don't know. There are plenty of different ways for them to work around the kinds of attacks we put them through," Kortez countered. "If we're going to hit them hard, I'd like it if we did it in a way that didn't end up with us giving them the chance to adapt to our attack."

The worst part was that it looked like the mutants were already adapting to the changes. She saw a spike in the temperatures around them to the point where the ice was already starting to melt, filling the room with mist.

Not enough to change their visibility, but she felt like it might obscure something moving out there.

"I think I preferred the ice," Chill whispered, pointing her rifle at where she thought she saw movement. It was whisps of steam moving in a gust of wind. "You think this is going to bring the fuckers back to life?"

The answer to the question became apparent. Creepers pushed away from the wall. A few of them left chunks behind. They were all moving like their blood was still partially frozen.

Chill had no idea how they could be anything but dead, but they were finding that the infection did unnatural things. If it could allow a Dahin to go toe-to-toe with the suits the Janissaries wore, she couldn't put limitations on what they were up against.

She fired at the closest one and watched the rounds rip through the bodies, which were more fragile than usual. It made them a lot easier to turn into mush before the creatures could attack.

Still, it looked like they were going to face more resistance as they continued forward. The film was spreading constantly, and the infrared readers on their HUDs marked it as the source of the sudden heat spike. It was fighting the chill that had taken over the chamber.

"How many of the creepers do you think are in the walls?" Ivan asked, picking off another one as it stepped out of the prefab.

"You remember how many we picked up using the sensors?" Chill reminded him, raising an eyebrow. "We assumed they were about packed in like bots, waiting to be activated and sent out to swarm us."

"Right."

"How many of those creepers we picked up on the sensors are the ones we're looking at, stuck in the walls like that?"

Ivan got what she was talking about. Chill had been trying not to think about it since they saw the creatures stacked against the walls. As it turned out, they were walking into the middle of the kind of disaster that made the Scourge's nests seem like a leisurely stroll through a park.

None of them wanted to say it, but Chill was aware that they had to move faster. They'd created a buffer between them and the overwhelming numbers the mutants could bring to bear on intruders, but the buffer was disappearing much faster than they had anticipated.

Chill picked another creeper off. It had ice crystals jutting from its chest. Another was frozen to a creeper beside it. For a moment, she thought the creeper had eight limbs instead of four. Then one of them broke away from the other. It tore a chunk out of the chest of its comrade as they rushed over to where Kortez was working the next door open.

The mist was a lot worse in the next chamber. The flash-freezing of the area had somehow turned it into a foggy rainforest.

"Straight out of a Giger-fucking-nightmare," Ivan whispered.

They had stopped in front of the door to decide what they were going to do next.

"What nightmare was that?" Chill asked, raising an eyebrow, not bothering to hide that she had no idea what their next move should be.

"You know, Giger? An old-Earth artist. Did shit like this. He's apparently very popular even now."

Chill tilted her head. "He must have been to last for this long. And the asshole made up shit like this?"

Kortez nodded slowly. "I'm as stumped as you are. I remember watching a vid about him a few years ago. The holos were the owner's prized possessions, worth trillions of creds."

"We might have to stop by and relieve him of them when we're done with this place," Ivan commented. "I don't see why anyone would want anything to do with artwork about mist-drenched rainforests in space filled with killer monsters and a bioweapon capable of infecting an entire station without breaking a sweat."

"Art has never been my strength," Chill muttered. She took a tentative step forward with her hammer and rifle at the ready in case anything used the mist to launch a surprise attack. She would prefer to use the rifle, yet if something got close enough to attack, it would be met by her hammer with enough enthusiasm to show the rest how bad an idea it was. Not that they would care about that kind of warning. "Still, if they're worth a lot, there are plenty of people who would pay a fortune to glance at them."

"And you can find those people?" Ivan asked, jumping up and down in his suit to test the grav situation. It looked fine to her, but since he kept his knives in their baldric, there was still something wrong.

"Nobody can hide from me, although people who can be the middlemen on that kind of trade will be hard to find," Chill answered.

"Why would we need a middleman?" Kortez asked.

"For one thing, middlemen comprise about eighty percent of the population in the galaxy," Chill growled. "They get very crabby if you cut them out. If that doesn't convince you, it's good to remember that the kind of people who can afford an eight-trillion-cred piece of art can also hire a small army of mercs to take what we're trying to sell by force. It's a good idea to keep as a buffer between us and those shits."

They couldn't stall any longer. The other teams were reporting increasingly stiff resistance. They had a mission to conduct while everyone else distracted the bulk of the mutant forces. The Janissaries were leading those crews, adding their firepower to each advance troop. They would fortify the positions they took up when they eventually needed to retreat too.

"You really think we're going to find something in this mess and get the alpha strain?" Ivan growled as they moved through the ever-thickening mist.

"If we don't, we know what the deckies will choose." Chill pushed aside roots that were reaching down to where they were standing. Nothing was strong enough to stop them, but it seemed like the plants were reaching for them. "They're going to fight this battle, no matter how it goes and what dangers they'll face."

It wasn't going to end well for anyone. Chill had to find the alpha strain. If they weren't successful, they would be dead a lot sooner than the rest of the crews.

If that was how it trended, she would tell Dorian to take the ship and get the hell out. There would be no hard feelings. There was no point in forcing him and Ibu to die for no reason. If they could get away, they should. If they saved her crew before they left, she would be eternally grateful.

For a month, maybe. Dorian would remember that they'd saved his life when they first met, despite his best attempts to get himself killed. He would still be paying for that for a while.

"If the deckies choose to fight, are we going to fight with them?" Ivan asked. "We have some firepower on our side, but the five of us won't amount to much when it comes to this kind of fighting."

Chill started to remind him that they'd promised to fight alongside the deckies no matter what but held back.

She would help them survive the onslaught. There was no point in lowering morale by reminding him that they had committed to fighting and dying alongside the deckies.

She intended to do that, but she wouldn't force her people to.

All she could do was direct them to keep moving through the thickening underbrush. The deeper they went, the harder it got to see where they were going. The sensor data gave them a rough idea of where to look for the alpha strain, but it didn't tell them what they were looking for.

If they ran into one of the clones, they would be in the fight of their lives, but even if they won, they might not get their hands on the alpha strain. They would be looking for something more sustainable. The sensors told them there was something to that effect ahead of them.

She had a feeling it would be the incubation template the clones were being grown from. Most modern cloning devices called for growing vats, but those generally ended up providing inferior copies by the second or even the first generation. That was why they needed a few more advances in technology before they could be used on a larger scale.

It didn't help to know they were wandering right into the middle of thousands of creepers just waiting to join the fighting.

"I have a bad feeling about this," Kortez growled as they neared a point where the mist was almost too thick to see through. Even their sensors couldn't tell them what they were walking into. There were too many signatures around them to know what was what.

Chill stepped into an opening in the greenery. Something was blooming in the center, a massive tree whose branches reached out and drooped, covering the whole area.

"What the hell are those?"

She followed Kortez's highlight on her HUD and saw something hanging from the branches of the tree. It looked like fruit. It was definitely organic buildup from the tree, but it was a couple of meters tall and wide enough to contain something large.

"A seed, at a glance," Chill muttered, zooming in and scanning the closest one. There were a lot more spread out across the branches, making the pods difficult to ignore as they continued moving through the thick mist. The closest one was the only one they could use their scanners on. "Maybe an egg."

"An egg, huh?" Ivan shuddered inside his suit, getting a reaction from the sensors. "Don't suppose we should shoot them so they don't hatch and kill us all?"

"Whatever's in those eggs might be what we're looking for." Chill approached the first one to study it. The opaque skin was a few centimeters thick and clearly contained a thick and fleshy interior. "Dorian, can you connect me with Zichix? We've found…well, something."

"Relaying the message now."

Chill moved closer to inspect the outer shell of the fruit or egg. Whatever was inside wasn't moving. She would consider that a boon. Besides that, she wasn't picking the signals that told them where the mutants were.

"Chill, Dorian said you needed my help?" Zichix called through static, relayed as their comms were.

"Just need a confirmation on what's inside these things."

Chill connected her HUD to the comm to let Zichix see what she was seeing. "Never seen anything like it. Do you think it could be a source of the alpha strain?"

"Can't know until you know what's inside."

She'd thought that would be the answer. She'd hoped they could detach the fruit or egg from the tree and get it back to the ship, nice and easy, with little trouble and all the alpha strain they needed to get the cure going. No such luck, not yet, anyway.

Chill leaned in closer and ran another scan, but all she could pick up was what the skin was made of, and there was nothing conclusive.

"Fucking… Okay, I think I can do this," she murmured, hooking the hammer to her belt and drawing her knife. She pressed the point into the skin and drove it in as gently as she could, trying to get a look at what was inside without disturbing anything.

A thick, milky-green fluid seeped out of the hole she'd made in the skin. Chill twisted the blade before running another scan.

"All right," Zichix called, muttering something under his breath. "I'm picking up trace amounts of the alpha strain. Maybe whatever is inside is maintained by the fluid, and it's leaking into the fluid. I won't know until I get a closer look."

"We can't just drag it out if we don't know what's inside," Chill growled. "We're going to need to go in deeper. If it's what we need, we can grab one of the other eggs and get the fuck out of here."

For all she knew, cutting into one of the damn things

would alert the rest of the mutants and put them under attack.

She didn't want to risk it, but they didn't have a choice. She pressed the knife in deeper, opening the skin. More fluid drained from inside, pouring out onto the ground, followed by something solid that splattered.

"It's one of the clones," Kortez growled, taking a step forward and nudging the lump of meat with his boot. "Doesn't look like it's fully formed yet."

"I guess that answers our questions." Ivan nodded. "Let's cut one of these bastards off and head back to the ship."

Chill nodded, but something felt wrong. She wasn't sure what it was, or why she was getting the bad feeling, but it was a lot worse than what they'd been dealing with before.

It was familiar too. A shudder came up through her spine as she turned around. Something massive was moving through the trees.

Not through the trees. No, the *tree* was moving. Slowly at first but picking up speed, moving more fluidly the more it moved. The trunk twisted around to look at them.

The structure was familiar. Chill thought she'd seen something like it, but for the life of her, she couldn't remember where.

All thoughts on where she had seen the structure before were pushed aside when she saw what it was that was turning to face them.

The tree looked like it had been stitched together from three or four different trees in an unnatural connection at the very center.

As it turned to face them, it became apparent what was

holding the sections together was a body or parts of one. She realized what they were looking at.

"Fucking hells," Chill whispered, taking a step forward. "That looks like Lugosh."

And not like any of the clones, which were too covered in greenery to see more than a passing resemblance. All that remained was Lugosh's face and part of his torso. It had been spread to connect to the various trunks of the trees around it, making it difficult to identify where the body ended and the mutation began.

Creepers extended from the body, giving it something like limbs. Once again, it was difficult to tell where one ended and another began, with chunks of greenery pulling the body forward.

Suddenly, Chill remembered where she had seen the likes before. The massive beasts inside the Scourge nests, the ones that she'd assumed were just there to defend it, had matched what they were looking at.

They'd assumed they were part of the Scourge, maybe a last-ditch defense, but they were realizing that not everything about those bots was what it had seemed. It was hard to tell, but it was possible that the nests had been set up over bodies to contain and isolate them from the rest of the mutants.

Chill was willing to bet creds on that being the case. They had accidentally wrecked other pieces of Lugosh's body, which had been spread out over the station.

"I'm assuming the fact that you haven't brought a whole swarm of your creepers down on us means you don't want us to die just yet, huh?" Chill asked. She took a step forward, trying to seem more courageous than she felt.

"Nothing would make me happier than to kill you before you can call your little friends in to help, but if you want to say your piece, go ahead. Don't bother pretending you don't understand what I'm saying, old man."

The face tilted slightly and a smile appeared, showing off the creature's rows of needle-like teeth. They were somehow still intact.

"Sharper you are than the other pitiables."

It spoke with a thick accent and a breathy tone, although she wasn't sure how it was that it could speak when it didn't appear to have a functional voice box…or lungs.

"I'd be a lot more flattered if the compliment wasn't coming from a face embedded in infected trees," Chill pointed out. "Or if it wasn't coming from the asshole responsible for killing so many people."

"Kill? Never kill. Live on forever if it wasn't for interlopers. I give them eternal life, and you would deprive them of it."

"Living forever as your slaves," Chill growled.

"Slaves? All are slaves. None who would live forever, stronger and more powerful for the rest of lives." The head shook. "I give it to them and all who seek it of me on my station."

Chill scowled. "You were looking for a cure once. A way out of the infestation you were exposed to. I guess you gave up on that."

"No cure if it kills. I would die from this cure, so it is not a cure."

"Bullshit," she snarled, taking another step forward. "I see past the crap you're trying to put in front of us. You take control of the creepers, and they become part of you. If you really wanted to give them life, you would release them and give them a choice. We have the cure if you would just try it."

"No choice. They live on. My choice."

Whatever was left of Lugosh's mind was corrupted beyond repair. Maybe he was right and the cure would kill all the mutants. However, she was there to save the lives of the people who were still healthy.

For all they knew, everyone was infected now, and they needed the cure or they would all succumb to the infection like Lugosh had.

"Chill!"

She inched away, knowing what Ivan was warning her about. The branches holding the "fruits" were dropping. The skin split open, releasing the inner liquid and the creatures inside.

The trees around them moved as well, closing in and reaching for the invaders like they were trying to pull them closer to where their fruits were splitting open.

"I guess that concludes negotiations," Chill muttered, unhooking the hammer from her belt.

CHAPTER SEVENTEEN

Fighting a single clone had cost Kharkanaw his life. Chill wouldn't forget that. His sacrifice would be remembered for a long time, but so would the fact that one of them was enough to fight the leader of the Dahin Janissaries to a mutually destructive draw.

Here were dozens of them.

Chill wanted to think they were making progress, getting to points the rest of the crews wouldn't have been able to reach. That just meant they were going to have to engage in tougher fights than everyone else.

"You know, I bet you there are a few merc companies out there who left Mugh-9," Kortez grumbled, tapping Cortador on the nearest of the trees. That got a reaction from several clones that were slowly getting their bearings. "I bet they used that rep to get work bouncing drunk assholes out of rich and famous nightclubs elsewhere in the galaxy. Boring but lucrative work, the kind you get to relax at. Working regular hours. Worst that happens is you get slapped with lawsuits by dumbasses who think you roughed them up too hard."

"Lawsuits can get rough," Ivan pointed out. "Won't fuck you up the way this kind of work does, but you'd get tangled in so much bureaucratic red tape that you wouldn't have the time for fighting."

"I'd take my chances with that," Kortez growled. "As long as we're not fighting the strange and the crazy the galaxy keeps throwing at us."

They didn't have a choice right now. Chill didn't want to worry about what was coming up next for them, not until they knew there was a next for them to look forward to.

The plants covered Lugosh's face and body, so they couldn't just kill him and be done with it. They would try, and from the way the trees were moving, Lugosh would eventually join the fight too. He was hoping his clones would clear out the interlopers without him needing to risk another part of himself.

"You think he's going to call in more creepers to help?" Kortez asked.

"You think he needs the help?" Ivan countered.

The larger man shrugged. "Maybe. We're going to take these fuckers down, and I assume he's going to need reinforcements. It probably takes a while to grow those clones. Otherwise, there would be a lot more of them to attack us."

"I don't know," Chill muttered. "Eight...nine...fourteen of them should prove to be more than a challenge. I'd take on creepers after that. We might need to relax, you know?"

Kortez grinned. "All right, let's get to working, then. Ivan, you're ready?"

"Whenever you are."

Chill aimed at the closest clone. The babies weren't quite ready for a fight. They were still staggering around like newborns, unsure of the world around them. Not the fairest of fights, at least not one-on-one. Still, she'd bet that when they had adrenaline pumping through their veins or their equivalent, they would get back into the fight quickly. The idea was to rile them up to the point where they wouldn't be thinking about how they charged in to fight.

Ten meters. It wasn't a tough shot, even for her. The clone shuddered and took a few steps back as its head splattered on the ground. It joined the thick muck created by the fluid inside the fruit skins.

Nothing was going to make the fight easy, but if they could thin the clones, it would be easier. Kortez and Ivan picked their shots well too, and two more of the creatures dropped to the ground, missing most or all of their heads. That seemed to be enough to kill them quickly and efficiently.

The reaction from the rest of the clones was as stunning as it was quick. They might have been struggling to wake up, but now three of their number were down. Maybe Lugosh was done giving them time to adapt. Or maybe he had been trying to get them to run away, assuming they would know that fighting so many clones with just three to their number was a losing proposition.

Maybe he didn't realize how stubborn and stupid humans could be when it came to standing their ground against insurmountable odds.

"Come on, then, you ugly fish-faced bastards!" Chill snarled, taking a shot at another one.

This one managed to avoid being decapitated by taking a round to its chest. It went through and caused a massive wound on the other side, but it wasn't enough to stop the creature outright.

She wasn't sure if the clones understood her insults. Lugosh did, even if he pretended not to. She wasn't sure how she knew, but he was able to track their movements through the station. He seemed to understand what they were doing and had even gone out of his way to get them off the station peacefully, which told her he—or it, considering that what was left didn't classify as a living being anymore—knew a lot more than it let on.

The creatures let out the low, dull roars that were the language of the mutants and rushed forward to swarm the three of them.

The first explosion caught a pair of them and split them in half. Ivan had a lot of tricks up his sleeve when it came to the explosives he carried. The mines were her favorite. They were set to blast anything within five meters to pieces. The blast was directed forward, which gave them a defensible position anywhere they needed to go.

A one-time wall, as it were.

Three more of the mines went off, killing off four more of the creatures before they realized what they were walking into. The rest were faster than she expected, smoothly diving out of the way of the explosions and coming back around. Chill opened fire on the ones trying to run around them and managed to catch one across the flank before it crashed headlong into her.

They'd killed nine in a matter of seconds, which was impressive. Fighting their way through five with just the three of them felt like it wasn't going to pay off as they needed it to.

The impact knocked the breath out of her, making the station spin before she realized that she was on the ground, wrestling with a clone for control. The rifle was out of her hands, and instead of reaching for the one holstered on her back, she grabbed her knife, growling and twisting her body as she jammed it as hard as she could into the clone's side.

It didn't get the reaction she was hoping for. The clone barely reacted to half a meter of hard steel slicing its internal organs. It growled and grabbed her head like it was trying to yank it off.

From the way her neck tweaked at the second yank, it might succeed.

Still, the knife gave her a better hold on the creature. It was difficult to do so otherwise, with the powerful, writhing clone wrangling and ripping at her. With a knife in it, she could keep her balance using the leverage.

Chill yanked it back before slamming her helmet forward and cracking it on the skull. The clone didn’t like her kind of fighting. She had raised her hammer and was yanking the creature in with the knife and readying herself to take its head off when something hammered into her side. She felt a rib crack under the impact, and there was enough damage to her suit to set off an alarm inside her helmet.

She wasn't exposed to vacuum yet, but it wouldn't take much more damage before she was looking at full exposure.

The knife was out of her hand, and the clone whose

body it was stuck in was still staggering, like the blow to its head had returned it to the state it had been in before they started shooting. There was no time to check on how the rest of them were doing. Chill was too busy keeping two of the clones from tearing her apart, so she had to hope Ivan and Kortez would be capable of handling the other three.

"Come here, you useless shit!" Chill hissed, bringing her elbow down on the back of the clone that was trying to drag her down. She couldn't deal with the bastard using her suit's strength, and if it managed to bring her down, that would be it. But if she could down it before it downed her, she could kill it.

It still didn't seem to understand that she was insulting it. She twisted her body around, drove the creature down hard, raised her hammer and, hearing a soft whine from the inertia generator, slammed it down. It was an awkward strike, with the creature still pushing at her hip.

A soft crack from inside the body told her it had been a decent blow. The clone lost control of its legs and dropped down to the ground. It wasn't enough to kill it, or even stop it from being dangerous, but it would be enough to slow it down.

Chill reached for her sidearm, drew the pistol, and shot into its head. It wasn't enough to kill it, but the creature fell back, far enough away for the hammer's inertia generator to pick up more power. It whined, and she crushed its skull.

"That'll wake you up in the morning," she hissed, turning her attention back to the one that was pulling her knife out of its midsection. "You want some of me too?

You'd think Lugosh would be tired of sending his bastards out to deal with me."

It didn't seem to be tired yet. It grabbed her knife and surged forward, blood seeping out of the wound she'd dealt it. The creatures looked different from the clones they usually met. There were roots and greens sticking out of them, but not to the point where the foliage covered them from head to toe. They could see the roots jutting from the pale, blue-ish skin, and almost every other part of the anatomy. Chill had never been curious about Dahin anatomy, but the clones answered all the questions she had never wanted to ask.

And the more she saw, the less interested she became.

She slipped to the side, ducking a wild swing from the clone and punching a couple of rounds into the creature's midsection from up close. They knocked it off balance as she twisted her suit around and caught it across the jaw with the back of her gauntlet.

It was getting easier to pilot the suit. Not that she was an expert, but her movements were smoother. When she wasn't thinking about what she was doing, Chill forgot she was wearing it.

The clone turned back around, trying to attack her even while it was off-balance. She stepped closer, raising her hand to block the knife aimed at her neck before slamming her boot into the clone's chest.

She knocked it off its feet, which removed the leverage powering those organic muscles. Chill activated the hydraulics in her suit and bore down on the clone, pressing down until there wasn't much of its torso left.

It was as dead as she could make it. Chill turned to find

Ivan tangled up with the last one standing. She didn't need to intercede. Kortez was cutting the head off with Cortador. It dropped, and he stomped on the head, then the body for good measure.

"I think that was Kharkanaw's problem," Kortez growled. "He was a great fighter, but he never did learn how to fight alongside the other Janissaries. When he got the opportunity, he rushed in on his own. These shits are tough to take down, but they're limited. No weapons other than their strength. Fight with someone else and you can pick them off."

Chill collected her knife, shaking it clean of the blood before slapping it back into its sheath. "There's also the matter of these little bastards not being up to full strength yet. That's what it means when they don't have all the green shit growing from their bodies. It makes them tough to kill. With less green stuff, they are a lot easier to take out."

Kortez and Ivan nodded, but she could tell they were thinking the same thing she was.

All three turned to face the source of the greenery they were standing next to. Chill didn't want to think about what was on the ground, and none of them wanted to deal with Lugosh anymore.

"So, should we grab one of the fruits and run off?" Kortez asked. "There are still a couple up there. I assume they didn't join the fighting because they're not finished forming, but they are chock-full of what we're looking for."

"I have a better idea." Chill turned her attention back to the central tree as it started to move. "We're not going to have the opportunity to take one of those fruits. It won't let us."

"We won't give it a choice," Kortez growled.

"Yeah. That's the idea."

Chill grinned as she saw the tree branches move, shifting until they looked like they were coming alive. They turned to tentacles as the trunk pulled itself out of the ground.

"We know where we can get the alpha strain we need," she whispered as it came up.

"Doesn't that remind you..." Ivan's voice trailed off as he looked at Kortez.

The larger man nodded. "Yeah. Those fucking things we saw when we were wrecking the Scourge nests. You don't think those nests were built on parts of him, right?"

Chill had worried that she was the only one who saw the connection. Either they were too slow to pick up on it, or she was going crazy. Either way, not great news for her.

"Don't think about it," Chill growled. Creepers were being pulled out of the ground by the roots of the moving tree. "We just need to get to the center of that big fucker, give Lugosh a piece of our minds, and cut a chunk out of him before beating it."

She could only assume the mercs and deckies were having a rough go of it, although they hadn't heard anything from Dorian. It was possible the kid was just too busy supporting the other teams. That, or something in the area was interfering with their signals. Neither possibility seemed too remote to rule out.

"I suppose things couldn't get any worse." Kortez shot down a handful of creepers who were halfway out of the ground. "Do we have a plan, or should we just rush in and kill anything that gets in the way?"

They all exchanged looks, and Kortez nodded.

"Charge in and kill everything that gets in our way it is." He grinned. "My favorite plan."

Chill liked it as well. It was simple, with plenty of room for them to improvise and toy with the details. She crushed the skull of one of the creepers as she stomped past two more, pushing harder and pressing closer before the creatures could circle her. That was the plan when dealing with the creepers and with the Bugz too. They were good at it, and the more time they put into it, the better they got.

Kortez and Ivan worked together brilliantly, creating space for each other without allowing themselves to be encircled as they pushed. They were working on a longer path and taking most of the attention from the creepers and vines, which were starting to pose more of a hazard.

After thinking for a moment, Chill sighed, hooked her hammer to her belt, and drew her knife again to hack at the reaching tendrils. They were a pain in her ass. She had no idea how Lugosh could determine which of the approaching creatures were the mercs and which were his beasties.

She really wanted to meet the people who had come up with the biological weapon they were looking at now. A weapon like what they were looking at could take over an entire planet in no time flat and leave it bereft of its locals, cutting off any attempts to reclaim the resources. They couldn't control it. The biological weapon would use those resources to develop a civilization of its own, as they were seeing here.

Chill sincerely hoped the person had been fired when they presented this to their bosses as a solution. She couldn't imagine the kind of problem that would require this solution.

"Come on, you big fucking tree," Chill hissed, drawing a couple of grenades. She waited for more roots to come up, pulling additional creepers out of the ground, before tossing the grenades into the thick of it, cutting through the roots and wrecking the creatures nearby. "Show me what I want to see."

It was like he was listening. Chill dove to the ground as one of the larger branches slashed through the space where she had been standing a split second before. There was no need to test her suit out to find if it could take that kind of punishment. It could not.

Still, it was good to know the dangers they were up against. Chill drew another grenade, an incendiary with a phosphorous payload. She rolled it ahead of her, carving a path as it threw off sparks that burned at a temperature in excess of what the trees were capable of taking. She took advantage by cutting down anything distracted by the flames, which were quickly spreading across the area ahead of her. When the creepers focused on her, Ivan laid down a line of mines and grenades set up to go off in succession. He wanted to cause massive damage in one go.

The explosives made the ground shake, which told her Ivan wanted to keep the attention on him and Kortez. It would leave her an open path to reach the center of the tree, find Lugosh, and cut off a piece of him. That was interesting since she was trying to do the same thing. Neither of the men wanted to deal with Lugosh.

Since she was fighting solo, it made sense for them to take on the bulk of the enemies. She could rush to the bastard inside, like how the rest of the deckies were drawing most of the attention elsewhere.

It was bullshit, but the decision was made. If she didn't take advantage of the opportunity, it would open them up to a counterattack.

"Fucking bullshit," she hissed, shaking her head before moving through the path they had opened for her. She opened fire on a handful of creepers that had rushed through the phosphorous, burning and screeching but not pulling back despite being on fire.

One of the branches swept down to catch her, but this time Chill met it head-on, using her weight and the speed of the limb reaching for her to hack the thing off. Then she pushed forward, running the creepers over without slowing down.

Most of the creepers were attacking Kortez and Ivan. The chamber was starting to fill with smoke, which was offsetting the thick mist.

Nothing was going the way she wanted it to. Worse, Lugosh could apparently extinguish the fires. They were starting to die without even singeing the leaves or branches.

The mutant trees were probably sucking the oxygen out of the air. Nothing else would burn if there was no oxygen to facilitate the blaze. Her opening was closing.

"I've got you now!" Chill hissed, rushing toward the trunk of the tree, which was still pulling itself out of the ground.

She maintained her momentum and slashed the nearest

of the outstretching roots. It split off the main trunk, and she slammed shoulder-first into the trunk.

She bounced off the trunk, which told her she would have to find another way to go about it.

"We'll just forget that happened," she snarled, feeling a jolt of pain in the shoulder that had collided with the tree. She could only hope neither of her comrades had spotted the embarrassing move.

Chill slotted her rifle back into the holster on her back and drew her hammer as she stood up using the trunk. It was moving faster than the others, but it was still rooted to the ground, which gave her a few seconds to decide where she was going to attack and how she was most likely to get something out of that attack.

Otherwise, she would have wasted everybody's time. They might as well just back off and join the rest of the deckies and mercs.

That wasn't an acceptable outcome. Chill snarled, twirled her hammer a few times to build up inertia, and swung it into the trunk. The impact traveled up her arm, and the tree shuddered. The blow took a chunk out of it, sending splinters flying across the chamber and taking a couple of the creepers down with the shrapnel.

"Huh. Didn't know you could do that." Talking to her weapons was an indicator that she was going crazy, but she didn't care. Her weapons did the heavy lifting and deserved her respect. She sunk her knife deep into the tree trunk as well, augmenting her thrust with the suit's hydraulics.

The creepers had realized she was the threat they needed to address. She yanked her knife back out and cut the head off of the one she heard coming from ten meters away because it was screeching. Then she twisted to take out more with her hammer. Ivan and Kortez finally made their way to where she was standing.

"What's the plan?" Kortez asked. He fired into the chunk she'd taken out of the trunk as she dug around for Lugosh.

Chill chopped down and hacked off one of the roots that was reaching up from under the soft ground. "Breaking through the tree to get to the bastard inside. Got to be quick, or we're going to be swarmed. Any ideas?"

Ivan nodded. "Kortez can hack his way through. You and I hold the swarms off."

It was as good a plan as any. Chill flicked the hammer to Kortez, who caught it by the handle without missing a beat. "Go for the middle. It's softer there, and you'll get in deeper."

Kortez nodded and wound the hammer up for another strike. The blow took another heavy chunk out of the tree. Splinters flew out, and they finally saw what they were pushing for. There was something pulsing the inside, but the tree was already starting to heal.

But not quickly enough. Kortez kept up the pressure and took out more of the trunk. Between the hammer and Cortador, he dug deep into the trunk.

"We've got more of the bastards on the way!" Chill announced. Either they were being pulled back from the attack on the rest of the teams, or more likely, they were warming up and being called in to deal with the attackers.

"Getting there!" Kortez grunted, clearly putting every ounce of power he had into each strike. Between the knife and the hammer, he was halfway through the trunk. He was finally causing the beast inside pain.

Pain wasn't the right word. The creepers, mutants, or clones didn't appear to feel pain the way most creatures did, but they reacted to damage. More than they got from the Scourge bots, anyway.

"I found something!" Kortez declared triumphantly. It sounded like he was breathing hard, even though his suit was supposed to do most of the work from inside. Maybe he thought adding power from his body would give his suit enough oomph to get through.

Chill peeked into the hole he'd created in the trunk. It was difficult to make out with the way the innards were writhing around, but there was flesh inside that thick wood. He'd even gotten some blood flowing.

Although they wanted to rid themselves of Lugosh, they wouldn't kill the tree. She doubted they could, not with the weapons they could bring to bear. They only had one option, which was to perfect the cure. They had an opportunity to do that now.

Chill reached in even though the trunk started to heal around her arm, terrifying her that it would trap her arm.

She found what she was looking for. Her knife dug into the flesh, twisting and yanking until she could see the blood flowing over her arms. Then she tore out the chunks she needed.

She'd carved out a piece of Lugosh's shoulder, and a quick scan töld her it had more than enough of the material they needed. Zichix had given her a portable cryo unit, the kind they used to preserve their food. It would keep the alpha strain from decaying to the point where they couldn't use it.

"I've got what we need." Chill patted the trunk of the tree

in thanks. It was working harder at yanking itself out of the ground. A dull roar came up from the chamber all around them as if the mutants could all feel the pain of their leader.

"Time to get back to the ship?" Ivan asked.

"You know it," she answered, keying the comm to reach Dorian and narrowing her eyes when Kortez hooked the hammer to his belt. "Warm the ship up. We've got what we need and we're heading back! Tell the rest of the crews to set up defensive positions if they can, but don't take unnecessary risks."

"Understood," Dorian answered. "The ship's warming up and will be ready to go when you are."

Chill nodded and took the lead as they sprinted out the way they'd come.

"You know you're not getting that hammer back from Kortez, right?" Ivan asked with a chuckle.

"I had that feeling."

She couldn't worry about it yet. She could reclaim the weapon later, but at the moment, they were in a time crunch. They hurried back to the ship, watching the walls around them. She wasn't sure how she'd missed it the first time. They were roiling and writhing with Lugosh's rage, and he was driving the creepers to attack, even if they were still suffering from having been flash-frozen. While they were recovering quickly, it wasn't quick enough.

She understood why Lugosh had not committed more troops to the smaller incursion. Dozens of fighters came in from outside, and if those positions were weakened, it would open him up to a lot more damage than the three of them could cause.

Hopefully, they could deliver the killing blow.

"If that isn't a gorgeous sight?" Chill murmured as their ship came into view.

The sub-light engines were running, and the guns fired at anything that moved in the chamber. A film of skin had covered the hole they'd made in the hull. The chamber sealed, and the creepers started to slowly come back to life, but none of them had the fighting strength they needed to slow them down.

Chill had picked up on rumors of something catching up with them. It was big, but it always disappeared after a few seconds. With the thick mist around them, their imaginations filled the swirls and shadows with vivid horrors. It was difficult for the sensors to see anything closer than ten meters away.

They would take a look at that. If mist was giving their sensors fits, the problem should be fixed.

"I've got everything warmed up," Dorian called when he could see them through the thick cloud. "It doesn't look like we have a clean way out, though. We might have to blast our way out."

"Sounds good to me as long as we make it quick." Chill came through the lowered bay doors first and halted, waving Kortez and Ivan in through after her. It gave them decent cover from the creepers who were trying to chase them down.

"Zichix got the scans back. He says the stuff you collected is exactly what we were looking for. We just need to get it back," Dorian continued. "Let's get off the ground, then it's out of your hands."

"And I can get my hammer back," Chill growled as Kortez passed her.

"Oh, yeah. Good luck with that." The man snickered.

Chill smirked, shaking her head as the bay doors came up. The ship lifted off as she turned around for one last peek into the soupy mist they were leaving behind.

"What the—"

She didn't get the third word out before something hit her hard in the chest. She was seeing stars and realized that she was looking at the ceiling of their loading bay, fifteen or twenty meters from where she'd been standing by the door.

Her chest hurt, and alarms were telling her there were breaches that would kill her if she ran into vacuum.

Thankfully, the door was closing. Nothing was in the way. What the fuck had hit her?

It was massive, swirling with chunks of greenery that grasped at the ship as the door closed behind it.

"What's going on?" Dorian shouted in her ear. "What the hell is happening down there?"

"Lugosh," she wheezed, struggling to get the words out. "Lugosh is on the ship!"

CHAPTER EIGHTEEN

She couldn't understand how he had gotten to them so quickly. How had he pulled free of the tree he was attached to and come after them? He hadn't brought it with him, only enough to make a nuisance of himself.

And from the state of her armor, he was a hazard. Her chest was going to need medical attention *soon*. Breathing was painful, which spoke to broken bones held in place by the first aid the suit provided.

"*Shit!*" Dorian shouted. "Alex, do something!"

"On it," the AI answered. The mechs that defended the ship while it was docked came to life.

Alex guided the suits to where Lugosh was standing in the loading bay. Neither Ivan nor Kortez was sure what to do about the mutated monstrosity. Firing randomly risked damaging the 'vette. They would have to make a decision soon, but with the mechs joining the fight, Lugosh was distracted enough for the two men to make their way to Chill and help her to her feet.

"How are you feeling?" Ivan asked, inspecting the damage to her chest plate.

"Like there's a superdreadnought parked on my chest," she hissed, drawing her knife. "We need to get that fucker out."

There was no time to come up with a plan. Lugosh suddenly remembered who was carrying the chunk of his flesh she had carved out. He tossed one of the empty mechs into another, causing more damage for Ibu to take care of, before turning back to the three of them.

Although pain lanced through her chest, Chill dove to the left as one of the crates came flying in their direction. She tackled Kortez out of the way as well. The crate Ivan missed without her intervention.

"You save him but not me?" Ivan growled.

"You weren't in danger!" Chill answered.

"You couldn't have possibly known that. We know who your favorite is now, huh?"

"He's still got my hammer. I was protecting that."

Ivan nodded. "Right. That makes sense."

It was a lie, but so was the assumption that she had a favorite between the two of them. She hadn't ever thought about it. The two were an amorphous blob in her mind. There was no one without the other, and they were both her crewmates.

That could change if she put her mind to it, but she'd never had the time or interest in delving into the issue. Maybe sometime in the future. Definitely not now.

Chill moved to the left and Ivan and Kortez went to the right, splitting Lugosh's attention as it went for them.

"Is there anything I can do?" Zichix asked, thankfully over the comm.

"Just help Dorian," she growled, wincing with the effort of inhaling. Vines grabbed at the crates she was using for cover, pushing them onto her to trap her beneath them. "He's going to have troubles of his own in a bit."

"Not likely," Dorian hissed. "I opened the network for Zichix to join me from the treasure room, but everything else is sealed up tight."

"Not what I meant," Chill whispered, jumping back and away from the marauding mutant.

Her mind was still spinning. She could only focus on staying alive and away from the reaching tendrils that were threatening to take over the loading bay. Thankfully, Dorian had the presence of mind to seal it off before they left, but that meant they were trapped in the loading bay with Lugosh.

Chill could only hope Ibu was safe.

"Oh, that's what you meant." Dorian grunted, and the ship banked hard to the right. Chill almost prevented herself from crashing to the deck, catching herself just short of a rough landing but feeling a yank in her shoulder from the arrested momentum.

"Fucking shit," Chill hissed, keeping her grip on the rail as the ship banked the other way. Kortez and Ivan managed to hold on as well, and they stayed firm through another couple of Dorian's twists. He was doing some fancy flying to keep them ahead of the defenses that were coming back online. Considering they were still inside the station, it was going to take some interesting maneuvers to keep them from being destroyed.

Lugosh had gathered himself. The banks had taken him by surprise and tossed him around the loading bay. Alex had managed to lock the suits down before they were thrown around, and they were shooting at the former pirate. Their aim was fairly accurate, but several rounds went wide and plinked into the bulkhead.

Chill didn't know how to kill the damn mutant since the rounds that struck it were just absorbed and healed over. They would have to cause massive damage in one burst to keep it from healing everything they were doing to it. Eventually, it would wear them all down, it was more than capable of tearing their ship apart to stop them.

Its screams and howls in a language even Dahin probably couldn't understand left their ears ringing, adding another misery to what felt like hundreds of tendrils reaching out to pin them down. The empty mechs were torn to pieces as Lugosh hunted for them. It was still trying to pick its way toward the trio even as Dorian put the ship through maneuvers that were making her sick.

Chill formed something resembling a plan in the back of her mind. They needed to resolve the situation quickly, or Dorian was going to have to think about dropping the loading bay and leaving them behind. From the shuddering and shaking they were experiencing, that option had likely already entered his mind.

It was technically a possibility, but Chill didn't think it could be done in their current situation. She'd read that the ship had to be docked for the loading bay to be taken off with outside help, which would let it be loaded and unloaded faster in port. She'd also read that in emergencies, they could launch it without much trouble while they were flying.

Alex would know, which meant that the AI would probably have to make the decision when the time came.

"Chill!" Kortez growled, swinging the hammer into the nearest of the branches and crushing it. Splinters flew all over the bay. "We're running out of options. What should we do?”

"Why is it that whenever we need to come up with a plan, you all turn to me?" Chill growled, gingerly massaging her chest through a hole in her suit.

"Because you're the fucking captain!" Kortez roared.

"Does that mean I can order you to give me my hammer back?"

"Let's not get crazy."

Chill turned and slashed through a tentacle as it reached for her leg. "All right. I have an idea. I'm going to draw it to the airlock, and you—"

"I think I know what you're going for," Ivan interrupted. "You sure you can pull it off? Oh, and it should not need to be asked, but I will anyway. Can you pull it off without killing yourself?"

"Not the time." She looked at her armor. "If anyone can make the fucker think they'll be an easy kill, it's me. You two can do the deed."

"He'll think it's an easy kill because it will be," Kortez pointed out.

"I didn't say it was not a gamble." She shrugged, and her body protested. "We have to do it now or find another way."

Nothing else came to mind, so they had no other option but to get into place. Once again, Kortez and Ivan fought together while Chill made her way to the nearest airlock. Locking her boots to the deck was the only way to do it since Dorian was still twisting the ship around.

Her need to spew reared its ugly head again when she reached the airlock, but she pressed the button to open the first of the doors. Leaving only one armored door between them and whatever was going on outside was the riskiest part of their plan, but Chill was determined to go through with it.

If she died, she wouldn't be around to hear what a bad idea it had been.

She pulled a couple of grenades from her pouch—shrapnel, which would not cause any structural damage to the ship. Lugosh was occupied with trying to pin Kortez and Ivan down. Alex had the suits distracting and ripping tendrils away from Lugosh. They were all struggling to contain the monster, which made it all the more terrifying when the grenades went off against the core of Lugosh's body.

They didn't cause any damage, but the creature focused on her. He wasn't in his right mind, or he would have known she was trying to distract him. Instead, he left Kortez and Ivan behind and advanced on her.

Chill was suddenly calm. There was none of the panic she usually felt in these kinds of situations. She ducked as one of the tendrils tried to collapse on her. Others hammered the bulkheads, leaving dents as she chopped into them. The vines writhed and roiled on the deck like they were fighting to reconnect with the body they had been removed from.

More came in to attack her, but Chill could see the former pirate approaching her, eyes glowing. She didn't realize it until he got closer, but he had wrapped a creeper around him to keep him alive and grant what was left of his body mobility.

He swung at her, taking chunks of the bulkhead out as she swept in underneath. Pain rushed through her body, but it was easy to ignore as she opened fire on Lugosh. Her rounds hit the body, causing only minimal damage. The knife did more, cleaving through branches and vines.

One of its arms grabbed her shoulder, lifted her off the deck, and slammed her into the door of the airlock.

"Simple interlopers think they can stop me?" The maddened face of what had once been Lugosh grinned at her. "Pathetic."

"You think we're trying to stop you?" Chill gasped at the pressure on her shoulder, which radiated agony through the rest of her body. "Pathetic."

It was. Lugosh had once epitomized tactical thinking in the galaxy. The Jindahin had brought fleets to stop his small band of fighters.

She believed that whatever was driving the mutants had picked him, knowingly or unknowingly, for the mind behind the success he was so well-known for. Yet, through its corruption, he had lost that keen mind.

Most of his body was still outside of the airlock. Only the arm was inside, pinning her to the wall and leaving him exposed as he peered at her. He should have known that. He would have, decades ago.

It didn't look like he was aware of what the team had in store for him. Kortez roared something over the comm, not where Lugosh could hear him. It didn't matter when the hammer whined, glowing with energy as Kortez launched across the loading bay and struck the top of Lugosh's head.

The force didn't crack his skull open, which made Chill wonder what would be required to do so, but that wasn't the plan. The blow stunned the bastard, distracting him and giving her the opportunity she needed.

She screamed to give herself more power as she cut the arm pinning her to the door. She couldn't cut all the way through, but its grip slackened. She pulled free and pushed forward against the advice of her body, which told her she needed to take a nap after ingesting multiple painkillers.

That would come later. She closed the distance and squinted at Lugosh's innards—his body instead of the creeper he'd wrapped himself in. One smooth cut exposed the remains of his internal organs. She let Ivan step in and toss a pair of high-ex grenades into the cavity, which the vines were already starting to heal, sealing the explosives inside.

A second later, Kortez hammered the creature into the airlock as Chill slipped out.

Ivan sealed the airlock and opened the external door.

Chill sucked in a shallow breath, half-expecting those tendrils to stop the doors from closing, but they had all been severed from the source. A second later, they heard and felt the dull, wet thud on the other side.

Then there was silence. Chill half-expected all the

roots, vines, and tendrils that had been cut off to suddenly come to life and attack them.

But no. They just writhed on the deck and eventually stopped moving, leaving them with a pile of drying shrubbery. They weren't going to take any chances with it. Every speck would be tossed out of the nearest airlock as soon as possible.

"Dorian!" Chill called, sinking to one knee and closing her eyes. "How are we doing?"

"Uh, I melted through the skin and got into space. All the fucking turrets were waiting for us. I'm working on getting back to Zichix. Are you all alive back there? You're not, like, infected? I'm not speaking to the great and mighty Lugosh? He of the powerful brain and the mighty treasure—"

"You can stop flirting with the bastard," Kortez growled. "He's dead."

"Ah. Right. Well, I had to make sure, and I figured he still had an ego, which could be used to keep me alive."

"Good call, kid," Ivan replied. As he helped Chill to her feet, he asked, "What's up?"

"I'll live," she whispered, gritting her teeth. "Ribs and shoulder feel like they're about to pop off, but the suit's keeping everything in place. How are you two?"

Kortez stepped in to help her too. "I took a couple of hits, but they mostly stuck to the armor. Hey, what the hell happened to Ibu? I thought she would be in the loading bay when we took off."

"I was."

They scanned the bay to locate their armorer.

"You're not a ghost, are you?" Kortez queried, looking

around like he was trying to convince himself that wasn't the case.

"Of course not, idiot," Ibu muttered. Chill raised an eyebrow when one of the mechs she'd assumed was being controlled by Alex pulled its helmet off. Ibu had helped them in the fight. "You three need to figure out what you're doing. You almost got us all killed with that stunt."

"It worked," Chill countered. She went to the first aid kit they kept in the loading bay, pulled her helmet off, and took some meds that would help her walk.

"You could have—"

"It worked," she repeated, gritting her teeth as the meds passed through her injured esophagus. She did get some pain relief for her efforts. "You think we lasted this long, the three of us, using the traditional methods?"

Ibu didn't have an answer for that. Chill knew their luck would run out eventually, leaving them dead or stranded with no ship, no weapons, and no prospects.

All their success was doing for them was making her more reckless with their lives.

No, that wasn't right. It was the drugs talking.

She gingerly stepped out of her armor. Their medic was waiting for what they carried to clear the station of the infestation. That would leave them little to do except wait until Dorian got them back to the treasure room.

Chill reached for the pack on her suit and pulled out the cryo-preserved chunk of Lugosh they'd collected. There were more samples splattered all over the inside of their airlock if they cared to swab for them, but she hoped what they had would be enough.

"We should dock near the antechamber in five," Dorian

announced, sounding frazzled but proud of himself as the ship finally settled on a course. "I hope you still have what we went in there for."

"Sure do," Chill answered, handing the sample to Kortez. It would be better if he took it the rest of the way. "It's up to Zichix now."

CHAPTER NINETEEN

"How are you feeling?"

"I'm fine."

"You should let me run tests."

"I said, I'm fine," Chill insisted, settling back down on the cot, which she assumed the Over-Keeper had been using. "The drugs are keeping me happy and more or less mobile, and for the moment, you have more pressing concerns."

Zichix huffed and shook his eyestalks before turning away and moving back to the centrifuge. He had added their sample to the rest of the cure's ingredients.

It was taking longer than she'd expected to get it working. Chill had half-expected Zichix to add the Lugosh sample to a boiling vat, and poof, like magic, they would have their cure in hand.

"You need medical attention," the Treasure Keeper pointed out as its holographic image approached her. "I detect eight serious fractures in your right rib cage alone that need to be professionally set."

Chill tried to push up, but the brace Zichix had fitted her with as a stop-gap measure kept her from doing so. "I've got this. Keep your attention on making the cure. The Over-Keeper's life—all of ours, really—depends on making it work."

"Naturally. I am capable of running chemical simulations while holding a simple conversation. I believe this is what you humans refer to as multitasking."

"A lot of other species refer to it as multitasking too," Ivan interjected. "And every one of them would tell you that the focus devoted to each task is reduced as you add tasks."

"Well, it is a good thing that I am an AI and capable of splitting my core functions without any loss of focus." The Treasure Keeper sounded too cocky about things. He turned his attention back to the centrifuge. "The first sample is ready for testing."

A half-second later, one of the slots in the device punched out, steaming. Zichix collected the sample and applied it to the air scrubbers in the Over-Keeper's cell.

"Here goes nothing," Kortez mumbled under his breath.

"I've always been confused by that statement," Zichix commented. "It's so pessimistic. Here goes something might be more appropriate."

Maybe the little one had a point.

The AI adjusted the controls for the cryo chamber Kuzratha was in, slowly and carefully bringing him back to the Dahin's normal temperature. As that was happening, he was exposed to the cure pumping in through the vents.

"The cure has entered the Over-Keeper's lungs," the

Treasure Keeper commented, showing them the live updates for Kuzratha's body.

It looked like it was having no effect, but a second later, the infection started to dissipate. It wasn't forced out of his body but broken down, which neutralized the contaminant and allowed the body's systems to get rid of the remains.

"That looks like a success to me," Kortez commented. "Not that I'm an expert.

"An unmitigated success," Zichix chirped. "It works even better than I thought it would. The alpha strain's ability to evolve is adapting it to the mutations the infection has gone through."

"Success indeed," the AI agreed. "By the time Kuzratha wakes, the infection will have been fully flushed from his body, to be removed through his urinary processes. Now for the second stage, introducing the cure to the station's centralized scrubbers."

The centrifuge spun as he announced what he was doing.

"You might want to do it fast," Dorian pointed out. "Shoviil's telling me that all of our attack lines are being hit with everything the mutants have to fucking offer. His words. He's also been calling the attackers fucking crazy, so, you know, something to keep in mind."

"Fucking crazy in general?" Chill asked, lying down on the cot. "Or crazy compared to what we've seen from them so far?"

"I… Hold on. I'll ask him." Dorian chatted for a moment before returning. "Fucking crazy compared to what we've been seeing. I don't know if it is the best use of our time to quibble about semantics."

"Don't worry. They're already adding the cure to the vents." The drugs were doing their thing, helping her relax into the cot and practically putting her to sleep. They would fade soon and she would be back to feeling agony with every movement, but right now, she could relax into the brace. "With any luck, we should get immediate results."

"How immediate?" Shoviil asked, apparently having been added to the conversation.

"We saw changes to the host body as soon as it entered the bloodstream through the lungs," the Treasure Keeper answered, calling up data readouts from the Over-Keeper. "Still, so far, there has only been one test subject. We should know more after the creepers have been subjected to the cure."

"You're filling me with confidence," Dorian muttered.

The cure that had been introduced to the scrubbers replicated itself as the infection did. That was the point of adding the alpha strain; it could combat the monsters with the same efficacy with which it spread.

It was spreading to other air scrubbers across the station, although the AI was prioritizing the areas where the mercs and deckies were fighting. She didn't think it realized it was supposed to save their lives, and she had forgotten to tell it. Another gaffe she could blame on the myriad painkillers coursing through her system.

"I am seeing positive results across the board," the AI commented, calling up data from the sensors they had tapped into. "As you can see, the life-sign markers on all present are increasing and becoming easier to measure."

"Isn't that a bad thing?" Kortez asked. "Means there's more of them, right?"

"No, you big dummy," Ivan corrected. "Life signs are picked up by detecting electrical impulses. We were having a hard time picking up on where the bastards were because they weren't giving off the same impulses as the rest of us, or they were giving off fewer impulses. Right?"

He turned to Zichix, whose eyestalks tilted to the side.

"That's an overly simplistic way of putting it, but basically, yes."

"So, what does more life signals mean?" Ivan asked.

"It means the sentient beings who were infected are coming back to the fore," Chill growled, closing her eyes. "It's the clearest indicator that the infection is being pushed out of the body and letting the host take control again."

"It's progressing fast, too," Zichix added, calling up the data. "It's being spread not only by the air scrubbers but also from one infected individual to another."

"The cure spreading like a disease." Chill cackled weakly. "That's funny shit."

People kept talking around her, discussing the matter at length and in depth, but it was merely background noise for her. She'd needed to get some rest for a while, and now her body wasn't giving her a choice. She was going to start the recovery process whether she wanted to or not.

Eventually, her body relaxed of its own accord. It was long overdue. Everything faded to black.

Chill wasn't sure when she woke up. It had been a gradual process. There were still conversations around her, but she couldn't tell if they were dreams. Then she was staring at the ceiling in her room, trying to decide if she was still dreaming.

Hints of pain when she moved that had previously been absent told her she was probably awake. So did her sudden insistent need to evacuate.

That was always the trap in dreams, but the relief after she attended to those needs told her she was awake for real. She didn't even know how she'd gotten back to the ship.

She wanted to believe that the parts of the dream where the cure had been synthesized and spread to the rest of the station were memories made foggy by the pain meds she'd taken.

Which, as it turned out, she needed another dose of. Her shoulder was in an air cast and her side had been braced to keep her from reinjuring her ribs, which was solid proof that she was very much awake and ready to be up and about.

Two elements had been missing from her dreams, although the details were already starting to slip her mind as she stepped out of her room. She carefully closed the door behind herself before following the hallway to the bridge, where she could hear Dorian and Zichix arguing.

"It's not like they weren't already here on their own," Dorian was saying. "They were on the station however long ago, and only then were they infected. That means they'll probably want to get back to their lives now that they're back."

"I don't think I would want to remain on a station where I had been enslaved by a biological agent for so long," Zichix countered. "I suspect many will want to head back to civilized space and start over. Hell, they probably still have family out there who will welcome them back. Great uncles or whatever who weren't lost on the station."

"I'm going to take this turn of conversation as good news," Chill said, surprised by how dry her voice was.

Zichix and Dorian both turned to her, unsurprised.

"Morning, sleepy boots," Dorian called with a grin. "How are you feeling?"

"Like a felid shit in my mouth," Chill answered. "How long was I out?"

"I kept you down for a couple of days to let your body recover," Zichix answered. "You needed the rest, too. There was lots more damage to your body aside from the broken bones. Some of it should have been looked at days ago. Still, I figured you'd want to be up and about for what's coming next."

"What's coming next?" Chill felt tired and dropped into one of the chairs. "Have there been any problems with the cure?"

"Yes and no," Dorian answered. "The cure worked well and spread across the station like you wouldn't believe. There were more than a few hosts out there who were too far gone to be cured, but most of the infected are making full recoveries. They're asking questions about what the fuck happened and all that. Telling them they were infected by a biological agent that kept them in something like a comatose state while it used their bodies was a tough conversation, but they're taking it well. Considering."

That was an interesting problem they hadn't thought about much when they were fighting toward it. If they did manage to cure all those people, what would they be looking at once their bodies and lives belonged to them once more?

"How's the Over-Keeper doing?" Chill asked, coming back to the matter at hand.

"He's made a full recovery, and the AI has deemed the threat of the infestation is gone," Zichix replied. "The treasure has been released."

Her eyebrows shot up. "No shit?"

"Not even shit," Dorian chimed in. "And, as promised, he's leaving almost everything for us to use. All he took were those religious texts. Apparently, the Jindahin have already been contacted about the matter."

"What kind of treasure are we looking at?" Chill asked, feeling a hint of avarice. She wanted to know the size of the paycheck they would see for their troubles. They were owed.

"Plenty of artifacts, like those religious texts." Dorian called up a list of everything that had been recovered, likely released by the Treasure Keeper. "Worth quite a bit of scratch if we can sell it. Looks like there are plenty of buyers in the wings. It seems all those Lugosniffers we heard about were sponsored, so when the word spread that we'd recovered his treasure, they crawled out of the woodwork to pick up what had been left behind."

"There is tech in the mix, too," Chill muttered, scanning the data. "Like the biological weapon we were dealing with. Military tech for the most part, unless I miss my guess."

"The Jindahin fleet has laid claim to those." Dorian displayed the messages exchanged by the Over-Keeper and the fleet. "They've made a lot of concessions over the claim to the Serpent and letting the deckies and mercs have their choice of rewards, and they agreed to pay a handsome finder's fee once those goods are delivered into their hands. Still..."

His voice trailed off, and Chill narrowed her eyes. What was he keeping from her?

"What?"

"Kortez pointed out that it would take a lot of creds for the Serpent to be repaired and livable again, so he wanted to ask you if the locals could keep most of the creds that come out of this. I mean, we'll be paid, but it seems like we could, you know, miss out on the score of a lifetime and let the deckies take most of it."

"They have been fighting for the station a lot longer," Zichix added.

Chill nodded. "You didn't need my agreement. Did the crew take a vote?"

"Yep. They all agreed."

"It doesn't matter what I think then, right?"

"I wouldn't say that," Kortez cut in, stepping into the room. Chill noted that he was still wearing her hammer on his belt like he was afraid she would take it back if it was out of his line of sight. "You're the captain. If you have an objection, we'll abide by that."

She shook her head. "Nope. This is a democratic ship. Means you all have a say over what we do and how we do it. For the record, as long as we get what we were owed for this mission, plus extra for the additional work we did, I'm more than happy to let the deckies use most of the creds to put the station back in good order."

"Oh, we're making a good amount," Kortez answered. He took the seat next to her and patted her shoulder for a second before he remembered how bad an idea that was. "I mean, not enough to buy our own planet, but enough to keep us floating around for a while."

Chill winced as she rearranged her shoulder. It would take a while to heal. "That's good enough for me."

CHAPTER TWENTY

The station was looking a hell of a lot better. First, the defenses weren't trying to kill them anymore. Chill wasn't sure that would change, but they wouldn't be near the station if it did.

It was impressive work. She was proud to have been part of the recovery effort, although there were now thousands of people from all parts of the galaxy helping put it back together.

Two weeks had been their deadline and they had met it, although the circumstances had changed significantly during that time.

"You're doing it again."

Chill looked up, surprised to see that Ibu was the one chiding her as she studied the screens.

"Never thought you would be against excessive thinking," Chill answered, motioning for their armorer to take a seat.

Ibu plopped into the seat next to hers. "So, the Jindahin are here, huh?"

"Yep," Chill muttered, peering at the individual ships on the screen. "Eight thousand ships all told, and over a million crew. It's one of their largest fleets, although for the life of me, I don't know why they would commit that many to control the Serpent. A fleet like that could turn a planet to glass."

Ibu chuckled. "They're not here to secure the Serpent."

"What?"

"Did you even read their messages?" Ibu called them up to review what had been said. "Here they're talking about taking over the station, but that's not the reason they committed a whole fleet. That's an occupation army. Plenty of ground troops. They're going through the wormhole to retake the worlds they terraformed inside, looking to settle them. Honestly, one fleet for what I'm conservatively estimating is a hundred livable worlds in there is a fucking bargain."

Chill scowled. "You've been brooding about this for a while, haven't you?"

Ibu shrugged. "There isn't much else to do except let my mind wander while I fix the suits, and there was plenty of work to keep my hands occupied."

"Sure. Sorry I haven't helped much."

"Please. You're still healing from almost having your body ripped in half."

"True." Chill smirked and patted her arm, which was still in a sling. "Although I have to say, Zichix is coming into his own as our medical officer. I don't think I've ever recovered from that severe an injury this quickly."

"Right. Besides, it's the other two dumbasses I've been trying to get to help. They made messes of their suits too, and if they want to join the outer repairs on the station anytime soon, they're going to have to help me."

She had heard Ibu yelling at Ivan and Kortez over the past two weeks. It had been met with a lot of yelling in response. The ship was small, and voices carried.

"That's... You guys were doing all that in good fun, right?" Chill asked, raising an eyebrow. "I don't want there to be problems within the crew."

"Nah. I know they've been working hard on other shit." Ibu shook her head. "We don't have anywhere else to be, right?"

"The Jindahin are mostly leaving the station to us. They're following Kuzratha, their new leader." Chill grinned as she shook her head. "Not sure I like his new title."

"Well, Overlord Kuzratha does have a ring to it," Ibu noted. "Can't be a bad idea for the Jindahin Overlord to owe you his life, can it?"

"I wouldn't go so far as to call him an ally," Chill answered. "He does owe us his life, so we might as well make sure he doesn't forget it. That being said..."

Her voice trailed off, and she looked at the Serpent as the Jindahin fleet approached the wormhole.

"What?" Ibu pulled out a pair of cigars and offered her one. When Chill accepted, she lit them both and handed one over.

Chill sighed after she took a draw. "I don't know. It'll take a while to put this place back together. There's plenty of work to go around and lots of problems to face. Keep an eye on how the deckies and the... We're going to have to come up with a name for the people who were cured. We'll have to make sure they all get along. I'm thinking of bringing up a vote with the crew."

Ibu nodded. "You think we can stick around and make more money keeping pirates off of the station."

"The job's been offered. Kuzratha has asked us to help Shoviil get the repairs done. It's not the best money, but it's enough to keep us here for a while. We're due for some peace and quiet, don't you think?"

"Sure." Ibu tilted her head, idly stroking her dark braids. "Can't say Kortez is going to like that, though. He's itching to use his hammer again."

"It's *my* hammer," Chill growled.

"Come on, Chill," Ibu corrected her. "He's not going to give it back. He wanted that hammer since those mercs touched down on the station. You're not getting it back. Best you make your peace with that and move on. Find a new hammer, or try something else, like a vibrosword. I could see you with a sword."

"Please. I don't know enough about handling the suit to walk around with a sword that could cut my head off as easily as anyone else's."

"Still. It's time for you to move on."

As Chill nodded, the first of the Jindahin ships slipped into the wormhole. "Yeah. Time to move on."

VALKYRIE

Have you started Michael's new Chooser of the Slain series yet? Book one is *Valkyrie* and it's available now at Amazon and through Kindle Unlimited.

What would happen if Odin decided to get involved in Midgard again?

Our world is tearing itself apart. The evil among us are ripping apart the very seams of today's society, using terrorism and blackmail to create chaos.

Valerie Kearie, mead lover and history major, joins the

mercenary company Viking, Inc. as a prospective business analyst.

Her first mission is supposed to be a cakewalk.

Tracking down a digital terrorist known as CLEOPATRA, Valerie and her partner Jacob Pinkerton need to figure out the identity of the elusive mastermind and stop the attacks before they are killed for their efforts.

Moving from one dangerous case to another, Valerie can't understand why she is loving the running and gunning aspect of her new job way more than any sane person should.

Then there is the obscure historical knowledge that she shouldn't know...and yet.

Valerie isn't a wallflower, but she is having difficulties coming to grips with the new abilities and odd thoughts that emerge as she is drawn deeper into her new reality.

Can Valerie figure out why she is changing before she lands herself and Jacob in trouble too deep to escape?

Start the adventure today!

AUTHOR NOTES - MICHAEL ANDERLE

AUGUST 24, 2022

Thank you for not only reading this book (and completing this series) but these author notes as well!

Repair Regenerate Renew

Sometimes, I worry that I won't come up with another idea. As we finish this series, what am I going to consider for the next one?

For the first two years of my career, I figured I was a maverick. I was running and gunning through series and working on the Kurtherian Gambit universe like crazy, creating (along with collaborators) additional series to take the stories into unknown territory.

At the time, my mom asked if I worried about running out of ideas.

Crazy talk!

Not so crazy, it turned out.

I ran into a problem with burnout and lack of additional reading that wasn't Kurtherian, and the creative well seemed to slowly be running dry. I have spoken to these issues in other other author notes, so I won't rehash them here.

The point I was (slowly) drawing to is that I worked out of it and finally realized that rest, relaxation, and additional input allowed my brain to do what it does naturally. Create ideas.

This morning, Judith and I were dropped off at the Las Vegas airport. I noticed a sign for (I think) a dynamic stem cell therapy place whose tagline was "Repair Regenerate Renew."

That's it. That's the whole tagline.

However, it was enough for my brain to come up with a new story idea.

We were only a minute from being dropped off, and I grabbed my cell phone, opened Evernote, and typed CONCEPT: Repair Regenerate Renew, and a couple of other words to remind me what the hell my brain had just thought up.

After saving the note, I slipped the phone back into my pocket, knowing I had a new idea. Which is good, as I've needed a handful lately, and nothing was coming to mind.

I often marvel when serendipitous chance happenings like this become full stories. Why? Because if I had been playing a game on my phone, that sign would have passed me by in the early morning darkness.

Because I was looking out the window, I now have a new story to bring you.

As this series ends, another one is born. Look for *Repair Regenerate Renew* in the near(ish) future.

I look forward to chatting with you in the next book!

Ad Aeternitatem,

Michael Anderle

MORE STORIES with Michael newsletter HERE: https://michael.beehiiv.com/

BOOKS BY MICHAEL ANDERLE

Sign up for the LMBPN email list to be notified of new releases and special deals!

https://lmbpn.com/email/

For a complete list of books by Michael Anderle, please visit:

www.lmbpn.com/ma-books/

CONNECT WITH MICHAEL

Connect with Michael Anderle

Website: http://lmbpn.com

Email List: https://michael.beehiiv.com/

https://www.facebook.com/LMBPNPublishing

https://twitter.com/MichaelAnderle

https://www.instagram.com/lmbpn_publishing/

https://www.bookbub.com/authors/michael-anderle

Printed in Great Britain
by Amazon

85638431R00155